Flying by the Seat of my Knickers

The Travel Mishaps of Caity Shaw
Book One

Eliza Watson

Flying by the Seat of My Knickers

ISBN-10: 0-9895219-7-4
ISBN-13: 978-0-9895219-7-0

Printed in the United States of America.

Also by Eliza Watson

Kissing My Old Life Au Revoir

Writing as Eliza Daly

Under Her Spell

Identity Crisis

Writing Young Adult as Beth Watson

Getting a Life, Even If You're Dead

To my Irish rellies

Charlotte, Alexander, and Ivan Molloy,
Bernard Bolger, Matty Nolan, Joyce Fullerton,
William Fullerton, Patricia Barron, Patrick Flannery,
Bernard Joyce, Des Joyce, Caroline Joyce,
and Imelda Abberton

ACKNOWLEDGMENTS

Flying by the Seat of My Knickers would never have been written if it wasn't for my Irish rellies and friends. Thank you for welcoming me into your families and for helping Mark and I make Ireland our second home. I'm eternally grateful to Katrina and Franz Molloy for discovering our house and convincing me that, *yes*, I could own a home in Ireland. If it wasn't for the hard work and dedication of genealogist, supersleuth, and friend Jane Daly, I'd still be wandering aimlessly through Ireland's cemeteries searching for ancestry clues. Thanks a mil, Jane!

I would like to thank my husband, Mark, and all my friends and family for believing in me and supporting my writing in so many ways. I would have given up years ago without your encouragement. Thank you to everyone who read *Flying by the Seat of My Knickers* and provided in-depth feedback, helping to make it a stronger book: Nikki Mason, Elizabeth Wright, Samantha March, Laura Iding, Sandra Watson, Kate Bowman, and Robyn Neeley. Thanks also to Sandra Watson for providing professional insight into

Narcissistic Personality Disorder and the damaging, emotional effect narcissists have on their victims. To my mom, Judy Watson (née Flannery), for sharing my interest in our Irish heritage and for understanding my obsession with Ancestry.com. I will forever cherish the memories of our numerous research journeys to Ireland.

To Lyndsey Lewellen for an absolutely brilliant cover. You are incredibly talented and understood my vision right from the cover's initial concept, making the process a breeze. To Dori Harrell for your fab editorial skills. And to Amy Atwell at Author E.M.S. for another flawless interior format.

CHAPTER ONE

"You want me to dress up like a piece of meat?" I glared at the foam costume, a bratwurst in a bun, covered with felt.

"The temp is obviously a no-show." My sister, Rachel, peered around Daly's, a Dublin pub, one last time for the missing girl, who'd likely seen the costume and fled. "The welcome dinner starts in a half hour. You'll just have a few souvenir photos taken with attendees."

More like *blackmail* photos.

I'd worked as Santa's helper at the mall three times. The green elf outfit had made my skin look yellow. The velvet collar had given me a rash. The pointy shoes had caused blisters on my toes, their jingling bells once attracting two stray dogs that chased me through the mall parking lot to my car. That costume had been haute couture compared to this one.

"You'll be dressed up. Nobody will even know it's you. Gretchen is on food and beverage. Declan is working ground. I had you as a floater. I need you to do this, Caity."

I plastered on a perky smile. "Of course I'll do it." As if I had a choice.

Per Mom's request, Rachel, an event planner for Brecker, a Milwaukee-based beer company, had hired me to work a meeting in Dublin. Mom promised not to tell my older sister why I'd been fired three months ago from my first job out of college. Between losing my job after only ten months and my past track record, Rachel probably thought dressing up like a piece of meat was the limit of my abilities. Maybe she was tired of picking up my slack for twenty-four years and upset that Mom had forced her to hire me. Maybe making me dress up like a bratwurst was her idea of revenge.

My stomach clenched. What else did she have planned for me this trip?

Rachel waved over Declan, another staff member on our team. "Help Caity into this costume."

Declan studied the costume with a smile, a sparkle in his blue Irish eyes. "A sausage, is it?"

"A bratwurst," I said.

"A banger." Rachel looked at Declan. "Isn't that what you call it here?"

"Only if you're English."

Call it filet mignon in a bun—it was still hideous.

"To celebrate Brecker purchasing Flanagan's beer, they've teamed up with Kildare Sausage to promote beer sausages at Ireland's fall festivals. This is huge for Brecker. And don't forget this meeting is about nurturing relationships with Flanagan's employees. Don't ever use the word *acquisition*." Rachel glanced at her watch, then over at me. "You need to get dressed."

Declan grabbed the costume off the table. Just when I thought I couldn't be more humiliated, I had a hot guy stuffing me into a sausage costume. My self-esteem had hit an all-time low.

"I don't need help. I can do it."

Rachel's gaze narrowed. "How do you plan to zip up the back of the costume when you'll barely be able to move in it? Besides, I had Declan down as the sausage handler for the opening of the reception."

At least Brecker had done a buyout at this Temple Bar area pub. Brecker's VIPs and top beer distributers wouldn't think this was as ridiculous as the locals would. The only locals included executives from Flanagan's and Kildare Sausage, who were responsible for my Dublin debut as a sausage.

Gretchen, a tall blond American staff member, walked up. "They said they don't have the Brecker Dark posters."

"Seriously?" The small vein in Rachel's forehead pulsated. Now probably wasn't the time to mention she really should consider bangs. Her blue-eyed gaze darted around the pub filled with Guinness, Smithwick's, Flanagan's, and other Irish beer and liquor signs. "Unbelievable." She marched toward the manager, talking with two musicians. Her black high heels clicked against the scarred wooden floor, and her short brown hair bounced against her shoulders.

Gretchen eyed the sausage costume with amusement. "You must have done something to really piss her off." She strutted across the pub toward Rachel.

I'd known Gretchen for two days. It had only taken me two *minutes* to determine she was a bitch.

"If it makes you feel better, these are brilliant sausages," Declan said.

"It doesn't."

"Won't be so bad. I've done madder things."

"Would you like to do this?"

He smiled. "No thanks. Think of it as your initiation into your new career."

"This is a one-time job, helping out my sister."

It was more the other way around. I was being paid a wad of cash I didn't owe taxes on until next April—well technically, January—allowing me to make a dent in my massive debt. Ultimately, I needed a stable, full-time job with benefits, and one I didn't have to be intoxicated to travel to. Flying sucked.

Declan looked skeptical. "Sure, it's a one-off job. Until you get bit with the travel bug." He gestured to my hand holding a postcard of the pub—a red exterior with black trim and gold lettering reading *Daly's*. I'd planned to send it to someone, bragging about my first trip abroad for my glamorous job. I stuffed the postcard in my back pocket, not having anyone besides Mom to send it to anyway.

Declan knelt and held out the costume. I caught a whiff of freshly fallen rain. Either it was his shampoo or he'd been caught in the rain while greeting attendees arriving from the airport. The calming scent caused my shoulders to relax slightly. I removed my shoes, then stuck my foot through a hole in the foam costume and slipped into the red legging, teetering on one leg. I braced a hand on Declan's shoulder, steadying myself, sliding my foot into a shoe five sizes too big. I did the same with my other foot. I wiggled my toes.

"How am I supposed to walk in clown feet?"

Although my new expensive shoes Rachel had recommended, since I'd be on my feet all day, wouldn't stay *on* my feet. The backless shoes kept slipping off, making it difficult to walk.

"Clowns do it all the time," Declan said.

Precisely what I felt like. A clown.

"Don't feel bad. I once had to dress like a leprechaun. I'm a bit tall for a leprechaun, I'd say."

Declan was a half foot taller than me, around five feet nine inches, undoubtedly much taller than your average leprechaun.

"And I wasn't hidden behind a foam costume, merely a bloody red wig and fake beard."

"Hey, what's wrong with red hair?"

"Yours is a nice auburn, not a bright, shocking red. And that wasn't even the most humiliating part. The meeting planner made me stand outside the group's breakfast every day and say, 'Top o' the mornin' to ye.' How mad is that? Nobody in Ireland actually says that."

I eyed Declan's crisp white button-down shirt and black suit, trying to picture him in a green velvet ensemble, a red wig messing up his wavy, short brown hair. His hair always looked like he'd just run his fingers through it. A very laid-back style, like Declan.

I smiled. "Are you serious or just trying to make me feel better?"

"Dead serious. Never worked her meetings again."

Feeling a tad better, I slipped my arms through the

red sleeves. Declan zipped up the back, and I immediately had to pee. Great. The costume's mouth provided a limited view. I turned my head, staring at foam. I had to turn my entire body to look around. The costume was top heavy, causing me to wobble when I took a step. Declan steadied me.

"Don't ditch me," I said.

"I won't."

As if on cue, the musicians started singing about a rocky road to Dublin. I glanced over at the two middle-aged guys perched on stools at the front of the pub. One gave me a mischievous wink. A real comedian.

Declan offered me the crook of his arm. "Shall we?"

I slipped my arm through his. "Unfortunately, we shall."

The dinner was only two hours, the meeting a week. I could do this.

Couldn't I?

I had to look at the upside. I was in Dublin, working toward paying off my debt, almost four thousand miles away from my ex-boyfriend in Milwaukee, feeling safe for the first time in months. Even though I was disguised as a sausage.

CHAPTER Two

"I once had to dress like Heidi on a Switzerland sales incentive trip for a food company." Gretchen raised her voice, competing with the trio singing lively Irish tunes and the tourists packed into the pub across the street. I could picture Gretchen's blond hair braided in a stylish twist, her breasts heaving out of a sexy, laced-up corset dress.

Where the hell was the bartender with my Guinness?

Gretchen's stories were undoubtedly meant to make me relive the whole sausage humiliation. As if I could forget. I'd had almost a hundred photos taken with thirty Brecker attendees and dozens of Flanagan's and Kildare Sausage employees. As soon as the dinner had ended, I'd stripped off my costume, peed, and fled to this pub, famished but preferring not to eat our group's cold leftovers. At least I hadn't fallen or knocked anyone unconscious while bobbing around. I'd made a damn good sausage.

"Wait, that was in Budapest, which was all the crazier since Heidi was Swiss, not Hungarian."

"Is Budapest safe?" I asked.

Gretchen rolled her green eyes. "It's Budapest, not Karachi. I've been there several times."

I felt like an idiot, not just because I was the only one who apparently questioned Budapest's safety but I had no clue where the hell Karachi was.

"I'm going there for the first time in the spring," Declan said, standing next to Gretchen and me seated on barstools. "Working a sales incentive."

"I'm so bummed I was already booked." Gretchen probably thought her pouty expression made her look sexy rather than whiney. "Their Paris trip was so much fun last year." She flashed Declan a suggestive smile.

What *happened* in Paris obviously didn't *stay* in Paris. If she started reminiscing about how she'd once had to dress up like a French maid for Declan in Paris, I was outta there.

"Forgot to tell you, I became a million-miler," Gretchen told Declan.

"A million-miler is someone who's flown a million miles on one airline." Declan saved me the embarrassment of asking.

Gretchen had flown a million miles? She didn't even look thirty, despite her constant frowning and furrowed brow. I had four thousand miles toward my million-miler status, thanks to Rachel signing me up for my first frequent flyer program. I'd only flown twice before—to visit relatives in Phoenix and to Disney World on a family vacation. I wasn't about to admit the most exotic place I'd ever been was Morocco at Epcot Center.

The bartender finally arrived with our pints of Guinness. If Rachel were there rather than at the hotel working, we'd be drinking Brecker Dark or Flanagan's. In the past two days, we'd barely spoken. She'd worked on the eight-hour flight from Chicago while I'd watched movies and gone broke on wine, trying to ignore the turbulence and my first time flying over thousands of miles of water.

Rachel and I had been fairly close growing up, until she'd graduated college and taken the job at Brecker, and then my ex came along, causing us to grow even further apart. It didn't appear we'd have time to reconnect on this trip when I really needed someone to confide in.

I snapped a pic of my first Guinness ever, feeling Gretchen's mental eye roll that I acted like a tourist. I slipped the Guinness coaster in my purse to really send her over the edge.

The band started singing about whiskey in a jar.

"To your new elite status." Declan raised his Guinness, his shirt cuff sliding back, revealing a braided brown leather band with a silver Celtic symbol of interloping knots. Very cool. Maybe I could find a similar one in hot pink or magenta. Although green was a more appropriate color for an Irish souvenir, I didn't own anything green.

"*Sláinte,*" they said, which I guessed meant cheers.

The beer's frothy top was deceiving. The thick, dark liquid tasted like beer-flavored coffee. Neither were my favorite beverages. I preferred wine. I'd ordered Guinness to fit in better. As if that were possible.

"I'm going straight from here to Amsterdam,"

Gretchen said. "Working with Paula Wilson. I swear every year I'll never do her meeting again. Her mom comes on-site to *work*, and I pick up the slack." She glared at me over the rim of her glass.

So Gretchen didn't like me because she was against nepotism? As if she'd be picking up *my* slack. Okay, she might be, since I had no clue what I was doing. But she wouldn't be such a bitch about it if Rachel were there.

A group of tourists posed for a picture with the musicians. Wanting a picture of me in an Irish pub and without a sausage costume on, I asked our waiter to snap a shot of us. We stood in front of the wooden bar with Celtic-patterned stained-glass panels lining the back of it. Declan slipped an arm around my shoulder. Gretchen gave me the evil eye, then cozied up next to him, flashing a fake smile for the camera. Was her issue with me nepotism or jealousy? As if I were after Declan. The fact that he dated Gretchen spoke volumes about his character.

Besides, a guy was the last thing I wanted.

We reviewed the pics.

"That's a great one," Gretchen said.

I stared in horror at the photo. The sausage costume had been a sauna, causing me to sweat off my makeup and my hair to go limp, my bangs flat against my forehead. Gretchen didn't have a hair out of place, her makeup flawless.

"Tag me on Facebook," Declan said. "Well, friend me first."

"I'm not on social media." Which appeared to make me even more of a social *outcast*.

"Ah, right, then." Declan nodded, looking baffled.

"If you traveled, you'd have to do social media," Gretchen said. "It's how you stay connected to family and friends."

Yeah, it was how you stayed connected to a *stalker*.

The bartender directed Gretchen to the bathroom—up several flights of stairs, down some hallways, and through two doors. Hopefully, she'd end up in England, unable to find her way back.

A dark-haired guy in a Jameson T-shirt passing by came to an abrupt halt, his glassy blue-eyed gaze narrowing on Declan. He slapped Declan on the back. "Hey, mate. How's the craic?"

Declan turned and smiled, then shook the guy's hand. "It's grand."

Craic apparently didn't refer to the illegal drug, or they wouldn't be talking so freely about it in a pub.

Declan introduced me to Kieran.

"Saw your mum this summer. Said you hadn't been home since Easter." It was the beginning of October, six months since Declan had been home. "Been a few years since I've seen ya. Not since..." His smile faded. Declan's eyes dimmed, and an awkward tension hung in the air.

Not since what?

Declan broke the silence. "Keep some stuff at my parents' and my brother's in London. My home is the hotel du jour."

I'd hate living out of hotels. I also wasn't thrilled living with my parents. Moving from Milwaukee to my small hometown a half hour away had been for safety, as well as financial purposes, so I needed to suck it up for now.

"Some big world traveler, are ya?"

Declan shook his head. "Mostly Europe. A lot in Ireland."

Then why hadn't he been home in so long? Ireland was a small island. A sheep could probably trot from one end of the country to the other in a day.

Kieran's grin faded into a solemn expression. "Suppose it ain't easy being home now that—"

"We should probably be off." Declan knocked back half his pint in two gulps.

Why wasn't it easy for Declan to go home?

And I wasn't leaving before I ate my Irish stew, or I'd faint flat out from hunger or drinking on an empty stomach.

"Oh, too bad." Kieran smiled, too drunk to realize he was being ditched. "I'm visiting my brother here for the week. Give me a ring. We can meet up. Still the same mobile number."

Declan shifted his stance, looking uneasy. "I'll ring ya if I have time. The week's going to be a bit mad though."

Why didn't Declan want to hang out with an old buddy or visit his parents? Was he trying to escape his life, the same way I was hoping to escape mine, if even only for a week?

Chapter Three

I arrived back at the hotel shortly before eleven, wide awake despite a pint of Guinness and a hearty Irish stew, since Dublin was six hours ahead of home and I was still jet lagged. I left Declan and Gretchen chatting by the door and headed across the lobby's white marble floor toward the elevators. Light danced against a crystal chandelier hanging above a tall crystal vase displaying red and yellow flowers on a glass-topped table. The Connelly Court Hotel had a very modern feel, except for the black-and-white vintage Dublin photos on the walls. Upon learning of my trip, I'd checked out the hotel's website, crushing my visions of an antique-filled historical building. My disappointment was short lived when I learned it was a five-star property, rates averaging $300 nightly. By far the fanciest hotel I had ever, and likely would ever, stay in.

A guy approached me—mid-thirties, tall, dark hair, and wire-rimmed glasses. I'd had my picture taken with him at the welcome dinner. How had he recognized me without my sausage costume?

"Do you know where the boarding pass kiosk is at?" he asked.

I didn't know *what* a boarding pass kiosk was. I assumed he was referring to an airline boarding pass. He'd just arrived today, and he was already making plans to leave?

My gaze darted around the lobby, unsure exactly what I was looking for. "Ah...the boarding pass kiosk..."

The hotel concierge was passing by and directed the man to the kiosk by the concierge desk. The guy walked off in the opposite direction, apparently wanting to be prepared for his departure. A bit OCD? I thanked the older gentleman in a dapper black suit and continued across the lobby. I was almost home free, the elevators in sight, when I locked gazes with Tom Reynolds, Brecker's CEO, drinking with several attendees in the lounge. He waved me over.

Heart racing, my first instinct was to duck behind a large marble pillar or towering plant, but I couldn't pretend like I hadn't seen him. What did he want? The only thing I knew was the location of the boarding pass kiosk. Not only did his CEO position intimidate me but also his confident and authoritative manner. He was late fifties, tall, with salt-and-pepper hair, and dressed in tan slacks and a blue oxford shirt. I reluctantly headed into the lounge, furnished in dark wood and red tapestry cushioned chairs and barstools. I tried to win him over with a smile.

He returned my smile, putting me slightly at ease. "What time's breakfast?"

I stood there dumbfounded, like he was interrogating me for Guinness's secret recipe. "Um, I don't remember. Let me call Rachel."

His smile faded. "Oh, no need to bother her this late."

Declan headed across the lobby, and I shot him a distressed look. He made a detour over to us and informed the CEO our group breakfast was from seven to nine daily. I flashed Declan an appreciative smile, said good night to the group, and fled toward the elevator.

"Best to avoid the lobby until you've memorized the meeting agenda," Declan said. "Take the second floor across to the other lift, then down to our office."

"Good tip."

"Don't worry. The job will get easier. You'll be grand by the end of the week." He gave me a reassuring smile, relaxing a shoulder against the wall, waiting for the elevator.

We rode the elevator up, Declan getting off a few floors before me. I opened my guest-room door and flipped on the light switch. My room remained dark. After flipping the switch a dozen times, I was about to head down to the front desk and advise the staff of my electrical outage, when a woman walking by said, "Insert your room key in the slot by the door. It controls the electricity."

I nodded thanks, having forgotten Ireland's green measure to conserve energy.

I stuck my key in the slot, and the room illuminated. I tossed my purse and black suit jacket on the red throw draped across the bottom of the bed's white duvet. A black-and-white photo of a 1940s Dublin street scene hung over the headboard. I snagged the hotel's white plush robe off the red upholstered settee by the window and slipped it on, relaxing in its velvety splendor. According to the slip on the robe's hanger, I could enjoy the luxurious feel at home for a *mere* hundred euros.

I booted up my laptop on the desk and Googled Karachi. It was in Pakistan. I had to start watching CNN. I then pulled up a map and located Budapest, refusing to let Gretchen make me look geographically challenged. I checked my spam folder for the dozenth time that day. Two weeks ago, I'd interviewed for an executive admin assistant job, similar to my last position. The interviewer and I'd hit it off, yet I hadn't heard a peep. The job offer hadn't slipped into my spam folder, so I checked my inbox again. No job offer and no responses from the thirty-one résumés I'd submitted. I blew out a frustrated sigh, dropping back onto the chair. I needed to send out more résumés, but I didn't have the energy right now, and rejection was getting quite depressing.

My travel journal sat next to the computer. I hadn't written in it since the flight over, but I preferred not to document my Kildare Sausage debut. I set the meeting agenda on the nightstand, planning to have it memorized before bed. There was no avoiding attendees the entire meeting when my job was to assist them. A very scary thought.

I slipped off my black socks and tossed them on the bathroom counter. Tomorrow would be day two for my socks and undies. Mom had washed a load of each last minute and set them on my bedroom chair. I'd failed to pack them. Luckily, Rachel had recommended packing an extra set of clothes in my carry-on. Today had been crazy busy with the group's arrival. Shopping was at the top of tomorrow's to-do list.

I filled the sink with hot water, preparing to wash my socks and undies with the hotel's lavender-scented shampoo. I eyed the other fancy amenities lined up on a silver tray, including soap in a purple floral wrapper. I glanced around for a price list, not wanting them to show up on my bill. Since they appeared to be complimentary, I had to remember to bring them home. Actually...I'd give them to Martha. The last time I'd visited Martha, a counselor at a women's crisis center, a lady had dropped off a supply of hotel toiletries. The women there would appreciate my little hotel luxuries.

When I'd finally gotten up the courage to leave my ex, I was lucky I'd had my parents' house to stay at when many women had to resort to a shelter with strangers.

I stashed the lavender-scented amenities in my travel bag.

I owed Martha a lot more than hotel toiletries.

I opened my eyes to total darkness. It took me a moment to remember I was in a Dublin hotel room, not at home. The clock on the nightstand read 2:00 a.m. Damn jet lag.

A noise sounded at my door. I bolted upright.

Someone was trying to break into my room.

My ex had found me.

Heart racing, I called the hotel operator and whispered into the phone. She assured me security would be right there. I hung up, and a voice echoed in the hallway, like from a two-way radio. I tiptoed over to the door and peered through the peephole at a security guard standing outside my room.

I heaved a relieved sigh. It wasn't my ex.

Still, it didn't make me feel real secure that security had been trying to break into my room. No way had he gotten there that quickly. However, maybe he was making his rounds, and had merely made a noise in the hallway, and my imagination was running wild, thanks to my ex. Andrew.

The mere thought of his name caused an icky feeling to slither over me. However, Martha recommended I call him by his name. That referring to him as "my ex" was maintaining a connection to him. I preferred to think of him as a nameless, faceless ass, unworthy of a name. Although I could call him Andy, rather than Andrew, since it sent him over the edge if someone addressed him by the *informal, unrefined* nickname. He would force a strained smile and politely correct the person's error while fuming on the inside.

When I'd broken up with my ex...*Andy*...four months ago, he'd seemed sane, trying to talk me into getting back together. Sadly, he'd almost had me convinced. That proved how manipulative he was and how brainwashed I'd been. After weeks of him calling, e-mailing, and showing up at my office wanting to talk,

I became a complete basket case and lost my job. Furious about being fired, I called and informed him that he had narcissistic personality disorder and he needed help. Despite my sociology degree, and a few psych classes, Martha had pointed out his issue to me. He became enraged and claimed *I* was the one with a disorder and hung up on me. That was the first time I'd heard him lose control. Even when we'd argued...*Andy*...had always been the calm one, making *me* look like the crazy person!

I'd thought I was finally free of him, until three weeks ago when I sold a painting, by a Milwaukee artist, on Craigslist, and...*Andy*...turned out to be the buyer. Thankfully, we'd met in a public place. Even after I'd changed my e-mail address and cancelled all my social media pages, he'd still found a way to stalk me online. He'd accused me of stealing *his* painting, causing me to second-guess myself, even though I knew damn well I'd bought it. He'd always played these mind games that had me questioning my decisions and abilities, ultimately my self-worth and sanity.

Angry that he was still trying to control and manipulate me, my survival instincts had kicked in. I threatened to have a restraining order served on him at work, hurting his chance of becoming partner at his law firm. I knew he was more obsessed with his career than he was with me. And I figured the mere threat of a restraining order was a wiser choice than actually filing one, giving him nothing to lose. He'd remained eerily calm with a strange look in his eyes and said, *You'll regret leaving me.*

Despite his stalking, I hadn't taken his remark as a

physical threat but rather that I'd have regrets because he was such a *great* catch. I still hadn't believed he'd jeopardize his job. However, when I'd recounted the incident to Martha, she'd warned me to be careful, that you never knew what a person like him was capable of doing. Martha undoubtedly *knew*, since she worked at a women's shelter. Her warning had haunted me for days, and his remark played over in my mind, becoming more threatening and the strange look in his eyes more psychotic. I hadn't seen him since that day, yet sometimes I could still feel those crazy eyes watching me. But he couldn't have found me in Dublin. I was overreacting, alone in a hotel room, in a foreign country, in the dead of night.

I noticed the door's security lock wasn't on and slipped it in place. I pushed the desk chair in front of the door, along with the garbage can, my suitcase, and anything else not bolted down. I rifled through the dresser drawer for the pepper spray Mom had bought me after...*Andy's*...stalking had gotten me fired. Her sister Dottie had been mugged while studying abroad in London thirty-one years ago, so she'd insisted I pack it.

I stared at the small pink spray bottle in my hand. I'd packed defense spray but forgotten undies and socks. I let out a nervous giggle, somehow finding humor in the situation. *Get a grip.* Mom and Martha meant well, but they were making me unnecessarily paranoid.

Weren't they?

CHAPTER FOUR

I squinted back the faint daylight encroaching on my room through the open drapes. My stomach tossed, my head throbbed. Not only from the Guinness, but after the 2:00 a.m. security breach, I hadn't fallen back to sleep until close to four.

Wait a sec. Daylight? What time was it? I grabbed my cell phone. I'd set the alarm for p.m. rather than a.m.

It was 6:00 a.m.

I was due down in fifteen minutes!

I flew out of bed, and my head about exploded. I zipped through the shower, washing only my flattened bangs. My hair was thick and several inches past my shoulders, so would take too long to dry. I threw on the hotel's velvet robe, then blow-dried my bangs and tossed my hair up in a clip. No time for foundation, I brushed on pink blush and applied my signature Flirty Fuchsia lip gloss, giving my pale skin some color. A quick coat of black mascara and eyeliner magically made my eyes look bluer and gave the illusion that I was well rested. I threw on my uniform—a black suit and a white button shirt with a red embroidered Brecker logo. I wasn't a fan of black and white, preferring bright colors. However, it made picking out my clothes easy when I was running late.

I scanned the desk for my room key, then rifled frantically through my small black purse. I was about to leave without the key, when I spied it in the slot by the door. I snagged it, removed the chair and my entire security system from in front of the door, then flew down the hallway.

Recalling Declan's advice, I got off on the second floor and sped across to the other elevator bank, so I wasn't delayed by attendees' questions, despite having memorized the agenda. I took a few calming breaths so I didn't look totally frazzled and entered the office, ten minutes late. I put in my earrings and blew stray wisps of hair away from my face. Rachel's red manicured nails were tapping away on her laptop keys, her hair flat-ironed and styled, her black-and-white designer dress crisply pressed.

Declan gave me a cheery smile. "Top o' the mornin' to ye."

I couldn't help but smile, ignoring Gretchen's smug look over my tardiness.

Declan eyed my shirt with interest, discreetly gesturing to two open buttons exposing my white lace bra. I quickly finished dressing. Gretchen and Declan went to open breakfast, while I hung back.

"I'm sorry," I said, sitting next to Rachel. "I was so tired after security was at my door at two a.m., I slept through my alarm."

"Why was security at your door at two a.m.?"

Ugh. As if Rachel didn't have enough to worry about. I peered out the gold-draped windows, through the mist, at the weathered brick building across the alley. No choice, I met her gaze and told her the story.

"I was probably just hearing things."

Rachel's brow narrowed in concern. She grabbed the hotel phone on her desk and requested the head of security. While listening to the supervisor, her hard gaze relaxed, and she nodded in understanding. I stared at the red-and-gold patterned carpet, curious what the person was saying.

She hung up. "Security was at your door because it wasn't shut tight and they closed it. My God, Caity, you have to be more careful. Always lock your door. There are a lot of weirdos hanging out in hotels."

Don't talk to weirdos, Caity. Reminded me of the time I'd wandered off in a store after Rachel had instructed me to stay close, and she found me talking to a strange guy, in the candy aisle, of all places. Her panic had scared the bejeezus out of me, especially when she'd broken down crying and hugging me, telling me she never wanted to lose me. If she knew I'd feared it was my ex...*Andy*...at my door, she'd really be freaking out. Even though in the light of day, I didn't believe he'd followed me to Dublin. He hadn't taken a vacation since starting at the firm five years ago. Again, *Andy* would never jeopardize his job over me. *Andy*...

A wave of nausea tossed my stomach, and I placed a comforting hand against my middle. I couldn't do it. I couldn't even use the nickname he despised without feeling ill.

Sorry, Martha. I tried!

Rachel had no idea that rather than incompetence, I'd been fired due to my inability to function while being stalked by my ex. She'd always thought he was a total ass, and he'd felt the same about her, using that as an excuse to isolate me from my family. Martha encouraged me to confide in loved ones, a critical step in the healing process. It took some women years to recover from the emotional damage and post-traumatic stress disorder, while some never fully recovered. I wanted to confide in Rachel, wanted to get better, yet I was ashamed to tell her how I'd allowed him to treat me.

Martha insisted I shouldn't blame myself for falling prey to a narcissist. He was at fault, not me. And that I also couldn't allow people to blame me for staying in an abusive relationship, or tell me I should be fine now that I was no longer with him. Sadly, many people didn't understand narcissistic abuse because rather than visible physical scars, it left deep emotional ones. So they were often unsympathetic toward the victims.

What if Rachel was unsympathetic?

"And don't be late again. Have a hotel wake-up call as a backup. I don't want Gretchen and Declan to think I'm giving you special treatment because you're my sister. If anything, you have more to prove."

Maybe I could start a support group with Bill Gates's and Martha Stewart's siblings.

"You want to grab breakfast?" I asked.

"I'm good." She gestured to a protein bar and herbal supplement alongside her supersized coffee. "You go ahead."

I met Gretchen on my way to breakfast, heading back to the office, with a bowl of berries. She gave me a saccharine smile, which I returned and kept on walking. I joined Declan in the restaurant down the hall from the lobby—a traditional pub with an ornately carved wooden bar and Irish beer and whiskey signs. The public could access it from the street when it opened at eleven. Still early, our attendees hadn't come down for breakfast. The scent of sizzling sausages and scrambled eggs on the sprawling buffet camouflaged the stench of stale beer.

I skipped the sausage, which I might never eat again. The label by the next chafing dish read *White and Black Pudding*. The contents looked like sausage patties rather than creamy pudding.

"Have you ever tried blood pudding?" Declan asked, appearing next to me.

My top lip curled back. "No, and I don't want to."

"It's brilliant." He snatched up a dark patty with tongs and put it on my plate. "It's a staple of Ireland. You have to at least try it." He placed a white pudding on my plate. "See which you like better."

I took a large portion of eggs but passed on the grilled tomatoes. The warm, mushy tomatoes didn't look real appetizing.

Declan placed a tomato on my plate.

"Another staple of Ireland?"

He nodded. "You need to experience an authentic Irish breakfast."

The next pan contained bacon. It looked more like Canadian bacon than the strips of crisp, greasy bacon I occasionally indulge in back home.

Declan put two pieces on my plate. "Rashers."

Wicker baskets held sliced loaves of Irish brown bread, with a variety of jams, at the end of the buffet. He selected a piece of bread. I stopped him, tongs in midair.

"I don't do carbs." I'd sworn off carbs two years ago. If I'd gained an ounce and no longer fit a size four, my ex would make a snide remark that *we* needed to start working out more.

"You can't visit Ireland and not eat brown bread. That's mad. You could be deported for such an atrocity against the Emerald Isle. Besides, in this job you never know when your next meal will be." He placed the bread on my plate.

A guy had never encouraged me to *gain* weight.

He poured tea into a dainty white china cup and placed it on a matching saucer. "And of course, no Irish breakfast is complete without tea."

I wasn't a coffee drinker. Occasionally drank tea. A diet soda provided my morning caffeine fix. But when in Ireland, do as the Irish. Declan escorted me over to a corner booth, carrying my tea. A couple walked in, and he went to greet them.

The blood pudding tasted like a spicy sausage, not as bad as it sounded. The tea was a deep golden brown. Delish. I eyed the Irish brown bread, then slathered it with black currant jam and took a bite, smiling in defiance at my ex.

A baby step toward recovery.

Following breakfast, I popped into the gift shop. My hand-washed cotton undies felt rough against my skin. I didn't want to add a chafed butt to my challenges this week. After being tardy this morning, and the security snafu, I wasn't about to ask Rachel for time off to go shopping. I hadn't admitted my inept packing skills. And she'd made it very clear when she hired me that this was a *work* trip, not a *vacation*.

The shop sold magazines, candy, toiletries, and souvenirs, including a pair of bright-green socks with dancing leprechauns. Thankfully, my black pants were a tad long and would hide them. The only undies option was a pair with a green shamrock that read *Rub My Lucky Four Leaf Clover*. Kind of racy for an upscale hotel's gift shop, but no way I was washing out my undies in the sink every night. According to my handy exchange-rate chart, they cost eight bucks, the socks six. Expensive, but it wasn't like I'd have free time to souvenir shop. These might be it. And they were necessities, not frivolous souvenirs.

I forked over my credit card to the saleslady so Rachel couldn't question my room charge on Brecker's master account. I wanted to save the fifty bucks Dad had discreetly slipped me, fun money for my first trip abroad, for a special souvenir. I held my breath, praying my recent $300 payment had been received. I no longer did automatic monthly payments, because I didn't know which bills I'd be able to *pay* monthly. The machine spit out a receipt, and I let out a relieved sigh.

After running to my room and quickly changing, I returned to the office, where Rachel, along with Declan and Gretchen, was waiting on me to review staff responsibilities for the day. I gave her an apologetic smile and slipped onto a chair, sweeping stray wisps of hair behind my ear.

"Gretchen will be meeting with the tour company about tonight's dinner at Malahide Castle and the day tour to County Wicklow later in the week. Declan, I'm going to have you see off Tom Reynolds. His car is picking him up at one to go to Flanagan's brewery. Most of the group is heading over earlier, which I'll also have you handle."

"I'm seeing off their spouses' shopping tour at 12:45, so if anyone is delayed, I won't be able to advance his car," Declan said. Several wives had joined their hubbies on the trip. "The cars collect them at the front, and the buses along the side entrance."

"Crap, that's right. And I can't do it. I'm meeting with the hotel then."

"I'll do it," I said.

Rachel brushed a contemplative finger over her red lips. "I could have you see off the bus and Declan do the car."

"I'm fine meeting a car." I gave her a confident, enthusiastic smile. I wanted a chance to prove to Tom Reynolds I wasn't a total idiot after not knowing the breakfast time.

"I know. It's just he's the top dog."

"I can do it, Rachel."

"All right. But this is really important. It can't get screwed up."

Heat rushed up my neck and across my cheeks. Rachel's lack of confidence in me made me look completely incompetent. If Declan and Gretchen hadn't already questioned my job qualifications, they did now.

I continued smiling, trying to remain positive. "It won't."

Rachel nodded faintly, not looking reassured. "I'll give you the details later. I'm going to have you shadow me this morning, give you some training. The vice president is stopping over for tonight on his way to Germany, so I need to check his suite."

I shoved aside my embarrassment and focused on the suite. How cool. I'd never seen a hotel suite. And it would give me a chance to watch Rachel in action, to learn a few things. She'd always been extremely organized and efficient, able to think on her feet. She was born two weeks premature. I was born a week late, after the doctor induced labor. Rachel had come out of the womb walking and potty trained. I'd been a late bloomer, walking at thirteen months and refusing to sit on the toilet until I was almost four. If I had a report card with all Bs, my parents threw a party. If Rachel received one B, a family meeting was called to order. Her punishment would be tutoring me. Maybe if my parents had set higher expectations, I'd have met them.

Always easiest to blame the parents when your life went to shit.

Fifteen minutes later, we stood in the seven-room suite decorated in black and white with splashes of red, larger than my parents' ranch house, which didn't have *two* bathrooms. I snapped a picture, envisioning Adam Levine shaking martinis at the wet bar while the rest of Maroon 5 partied with their groupies after a gig in Dublin.

Rachel threw open the curtain sheers. "Look at that."

I stared in awe at the River Liffey lined with brick and brightly colored buildings. A much more scenic view than the modern glass office building across the street from my room.

She shook her head in disgust. "Seriously, how can housekeeping miss a handprint right in the middle of the window?"

Because the housekeeper had been admiring the view of the Liffey?

Rachel jotted down the violation on her notepad. She handed me a VIP checklist with over a hundred items to inspect, including the thickness of the ironing board pad and the minibar for competitor beers. "I've found undies, a vibrator, and condoms—unused ones, thank God—in nightstands, cigarettes in plants, you name it."

We divided and conquered. Rachel checked five rooms to my two since I was being extra careful, not wanting to miss a smudge on a mirror or a strand of hair in the shower drain. A half hour later, Rachel presented her one-page to-do list to the front desk manager, who looked a bit overwhelmed but promised to immediately address the issues. Poor guy.

By noon, we'd made a run to the printers and completed numerous tasks. I was ready for a nap, feeling like I'd already worked a fifteen-hour day. This was Rachel's pace from sunrise to...sunrise, since she likely never slept. I envied not only her job expertise but her stamina.

Actually, I envied a lot about Rachel.

CHAPTER FIVE

I stood inside the hotel's front entrance, my eyes peeled for a black sedan, the car's license plate number etched on my brain. I'd been waiting a half hour. No way was I missing Tom Reynolds's car. He was standing outside on a call.

"Where's the bus departing from tonight?" a man asked, startling me.

I spun around to find the airline-kiosk guy from the night before. A better question, why wasn't he over at Flanagan's brewery with everyone else? We were going to Malahide Castle tonight—my first castle ever—but I didn't know where we were departing from. Was it this guy's mission to trip me up? Had Rachel planted him to test me? I suddenly recalled Declan mentioning the shopping tour left from the side entrance.

"The side entrance," I said, assuming all buses departed from there.

"Where's that?"

My phone rang. Rather than Rachel checking on me,

it was Mom. How was I supposed to feel independent when not only did I live with my parents, Mom expected me to check in with her daily? She didn't know about the Craigslist encounter with my ex, yet she still worried about me being in a foreign country. I'd assured her if anything happened to me, Rachel would notify her. Once she got everyone off to their meetings.

However, I welcomed her call. "Sorry. I have to take this," I told the guy. I hurried over and hid behind a large marble pillar to avoid further interrogation.

"Hey, Mom, sorry I didn't e-mail you—"

"They just took your car!" She sounded frantic and out of breath.

My eyes widened, heart raced. "Someone stole my car?"

"It was repossessed!"

Repossessed? I'd only missed one...maybe two payments. Didn't someone have to advise me if my car was being repossessed? Maybe the notice was in one of the many unopened envelopes I'd stashed in my desk drawer. Mom was at work when the mailman came, enabling me to intercept notices from collection agencies without her knowledge. I'd been able to defer my college loan, or I'd really be screwed.

"There I was sitting at the kitchen table drinking my coffee, and I look up to see a tow truck in front of your car. I ran out and asked them what they thought they were doing, and they said you're behind on payments and they were taking it. I said no way are you behind on payments, because *I'd* lent you money to *make* your last few car payments."

I knew borrowing money from my parents would come back to haunt me.

"I kind of used the money for some credit card bills." So I was able to make charges in Ireland.

"*Some* credit card bills? Well, I guess you have two less bills to worry about now. Certainly don't have to pay insurance on a car you don't have."

I should have sold the car, but it wasn't even a year old. I'd have lost a ton of money on it. Besides, it was red, sporty, and a boost to what little self-esteem I had left. I'd overextended myself trying to keep up with my ex's lifestyle and live up to his standards. He'd been the first person who'd had high, albeit unrealistic and self-serving, expectations of me. In some twisted way, had that attracted me to him?

"And wouldn't you know it, Margaret brought her garbage to the street while I was out there talking to these two goons. She never puts her garbage out that early. She was being nosey. I finally asked her if maybe she didn't want to videotape the whole thing." She gasped. "What if it's on that reality show your father watches? *Repo Man*, or whatever it's called?"

"I think you'd have seen the TV cameras."

"Thank heavens your father was already at work. He'd probably have taped the whole thing himself and sent it into that stupid show, trying to get on TV. He wouldn't even care that we'd be the talk of the town. He's obsessed with that show. So should we be prepared for more goons showing up and busting our kneecaps because you owe them money?"

"Nobody is going to bust your kneecaps." However, I hadn't expected someone to take my car either. "I'm sorry this happened when I wasn't home. I'm sorry you were embarrassed."

Mom let out a heavy sigh. "Well, Margaret certainly shouldn't be one to cast stones, especially when it comes to cars. Her son stole that car from the church parking lot last year, during service. I mean, who does such a thing?"

I glanced out at the drive as a shiny black sedan pulled up. Omigod, I'd forgotten about Tom Reynolds's car. I shoved aside thoughts of my red sports car being hauled away.

"I have to go. I'll call you later."

I raced out the door, and one of my backless shoes flew off. My phone shot from my hand as I headed toward the pavement, and Tom Reynolds said, "Holy shit. I'll have to call you back."

I lay on the ground, flat on my face, disoriented.

"Are you all right?" The CEO grabbed hold of my arm and helped me up.

I shook the daze from my head. "Ah, yeah, I'm fine." I glanced down at my burning palms, scraped and dotted with blood. The dancing leprechauns on my shoeless foot smiled up at me. Heat exploded on my cheeks. I'd thought not knowing the breakfast hours had made me look like an idiot!

"No worries, I'll take care of her," Declan said, materializing out of nowhere. "Your car's ready, Tom."

And my embarrassment intensified. Declan had likely witnessed the entire scene. Tom shot me one last concerned glance as Declan escorted him to his car.

The sedan drove off.

Declan walked over and handed me my phone, the

glass back a spiderweb of cracks. "Nothing some packaging tape won't fix."

It better. I didn't have money for a new phone.

The doorman handed me my shoe.

"Thanks," I muttered, whipping the stupid shoe on the ground.

"Brilliant socks," Declan said, eyeing the leprechauns.

I shoved my foot in the shoe. "You should see my underwear."

He gave me an intrigued smile, his gaze traveling down below my waist, lingering, as if he was envisioning my undies. Still smiling, he slowly raised his gaze and met mine.

My cheeks burned. "That didn't come out right. I forgot to pack socks and underwear, so I had to buy some in the gift shop, and all they had were souvenir ones, and..." I was rambling, embarrassing myself even more.

"There's a clothing shop up the street. I'll take you later if we have time."

Hadn't I suffered enough humiliation for the day without undies shopping with Declan?

"If you can give me directions, that'd be great." Maybe I'd be able to hobble to the store on my throbbing ankle. Too bad I couldn't afford new shoes. "Thanks for your help, but I'm fine."

"Ah, grand, are ya?"

He slipped his hands around mine and turned them over, eyeing the tiny pebbles imbedded in my blood-scratched palms. He gave my hands a gentle, comforting squeeze. I stared at my hands resting in his, a warm feeling washing over my entire body, not merely my cheeks. My shoulders relaxed, the throbbing in my ankle subsided slightly, my palms didn't burn quite as much, and...

Get a grip. A simple act of compassion and my heart was all aflutter? I slipped my hands from Declan's.

"Rachel's going to kill me." Since she'd warned me in front of everyone not to screw up.

I swallowed the lump of emotion in my throat, fighting back tears. I'd just lost my car and possibly my phone. I couldn't lose this job. Every time I thought my life had hit rock bottom, something happened to prove things could still get worse. I had to figure out how to stop taking steps backward and start moving forward with my life.

"Can't blame you for tripping, can she now? Besides, she'll never know."

I stepped forward and flinched from the pain in my ankle.

"Unless I have to rush you to the accident and emergency department."

Panic rushed through me. "No way am I going to the hospital." Besides the fact I didn't want Rachel to know about this, Dad's crappy health insurance only covered me if I was on my deathbed. Another reason I needed a full-time job with benefits. I was a total klutz. At only twenty-four, I'd already suffered a broken arm, two broken toes, and a sprained wrist.

"I once tripped down the steps of a bus while escorting a group of VIPs," Declan said.

"Were you okay?"

He nodded. "Luckily, the door was closed and kept

me from falling out onto the motorway at a hundred kilometers an hour."

My eyes widened. "The bus was moving?"

"Yeah, it was bloody moving. I was standing up front talking about the dinner. The bus exited too fast, and I lost my footing."

I giggled at visions of Declan tumbling down the steps and lying there, disoriented like I'd been, watching the road zip past, inches from his face. My faint giggle grew into laughter. I hadn't laughed so hard in a long time.

Mom had asked Rachel to give me this job not only for financial reasons but she feared I was sinking into a deep depression, after missing church bingo two weeks in a row and the Friday fish fry at the Elks Lodge. Was it a wonder I was clinically depressed when my social life consisted of bingo and fish fries with my parents?

Declan wore an amused smile.

I clamped my teeth down on my lower lip. "Sorry. It's not funny."

"Sure it is. If we didn't laugh at our jobs, we'd cry. Or quit."

I smiled faintly. "Are you sure you don't make up these stories to make me feel better?"

"I've been doing this job three years. Believe me— your stories could never beat mine." He gestured to my hands. "Although you might die trying."

I could see my obit now. Death by humiliation.

CHAPTER SIX

Two hours later, my palms had stopped burning, and my ankle was borderline. An ice pack would feel awesome, but then I'd have to tell Rachel about me tripping and be exiled to the sausage costume. Speaking of which, I was in our office placing photos of my sausage debut with attendees in wooden Celtic-design frames. My moment of humiliation was caught on film for eternity and would be displayed on VIPs' desks. I came across a picture of Declan and me the photographer had taken as a test shot. Declan wore a dimpled smile, and his blue eyes held their usual mischievous glint that made you curious what he was up to.

Declan snagged the photo from my hand. "Ah, grand, a souvenir snap."

I snatched it back. "I'm not having that show up on Facebook." Even if I didn't have a page.

Tom Reynolds walked in. I set down the photo and busied myself with a frame. Declan grabbed the photo.

Rachel popped up from her chair. "Can I help you?"

"I'm wondering if you could make a dinner reservation for Kathleen and me tomorrow night." He glanced in my direction. "How are the hands? You doing okay?"

I reluctantly peered over at him and muttered, "Ah, yeah, thanks."

Rachel shot me a questioning look.

He walked toward me. "That was quite the spill. Thought you might have sprained an ankle. Hope your phone wasn't a fatality."

Luckily, packaging tape had done the trick and my phone still worked.

"Sorry about interrupting your call," I said.

Rachel's curious expression turned to panic. Why had I mentioned interrupting his flippin' call? I hadn't been in the frame of mind to apologize earlier, and it seemed the right thing to do.

"No problem. Glad you're okay." He eyed the photos on the table. "Great shots. We should put one in the company newsletter with the article on our meeting."

How about plastering it on the side of a double-decker bus so everyone in Dublin could get a good laugh?

He gave Rachel his dinner details, then left.

Rachel marched over to me. "Spill? Sprained ankle? Interrupting his phone call? What the hell happened?"

As I explained the story, a horrified look seized Rachel's face, her breathing quickened, and the vein in her forehead about exploded. Good thing he hadn't mentioned my leprechaun socks. That might have really sent her over the edge.

"I'm sorry. I didn't trip on purpose."

I could see Rachel mentally counting to ten, like she'd done while we were growing up, trying not to lose it.

"I know you didn't trip on purpose, but I can't believe you didn't tell me this before I just got blindsided by Tom Reynolds. It's not like keeping Izzy's vet run from Dad. This is really serious, Caity."

When I was seven, I'd played with Rachel's Barbies without permission. I'd left them lying on the floor, and our cat, Izzy, had chewed off all their feet. Despite her anger, Rachel had remained calm enough to search for the missing feet, afraid Izzy had swallowed them. After tearing the house apart, we were short two feet, so Mom whisked Izzy off to the vet without Dad's knowledge. The vet assured us it was better for Izzy to pass the small pieces than to undergo major surgery. My punishment was being on litter duty, analyzing Izzy's poop for a week until the two feet finally materialized. After a few days, Rachel forgave me, and we took turns monitoring the litter box.

"If you hadn't been here and he'd asked how you were, I'd have been clueless and looked like a complete idiot."

You recommended these stupid backless shoes I can't freakin' walk in!

Rachel eased out a calming breath. "Are you okay?"

"I'm fine."

I was closer to finding a pot of gold under a rainbow than I was to being fine. Rather than this week bringing Rachel and me closer, I was afraid it might cause an even bigger wedge between us than my ex had.

❧❧ ❧❧

Rachel and Gretchen headed over to Malahide Castle early to make sure everything was in order. I took advantage of the hour break before Declan and I had to load the buses, and ran to the nearby shop he'd mentioned earlier. It was located in a brick building with red awnings over windows displaying scantily dressed mannequins in haute couture.

I asked to be directed to the underwear and was informed the *knickers* were on the far wall. Knickers were what Grandma Shaw had called my worn pants she'd cut off at the knees every summer.

I made a beeline for the undies. They started at a size eight. I had no clue how that compared to US sizes. The pair I'd bought at the hotel came in small, medium, or large. According to my exchange-rate card, these cost almost fifteen bucks a pair. Even more than the hotel gift shop.

My phone rang. Mom. What had been confiscated now? Outside of a pair of diamond stud earrings, I owned nothing else of value. I debated letting it go to voicemail. Not only did I feel bad she had to deal with my financial mess, but I had some serious guilt over us growing apart the past two years, thanks to my ex. And I always ripped on Rachel for putting work before family. I answered the phone.

"Well, something is going your way. I just received a call from the temp agency. Good thing they had me as your emergency contact, so they called when your e-mail came back undeliverable and your old cell number was out of service. Talk about great timing. So at least you'll have a job over the holidays. They said your position from last year was already filled since they couldn't reach you, but the elf job is still open. You make such a cute elf."

I'd forgone the elf stint last year to wrap presents at a department store since my ex couldn't handle the embarrassment of his girlfriend dressed as an elf in the middle of the mall, for everyone to see. Yet I'd *handled* the embarrassment for three years. The gift-wrapping job still required the elf uniform. However, I was hidden away at the back of the store and didn't have to wear the hat or shoes since the supervisor couldn't tolerate the jingling bells of ten busy elves. I was surprised they were offering me the elf job after I'd argued with a little brat over the correct lines to "Frosty the Snowman." Until then, my favorite part of the job had been entertaining kids with Christmas carols. Guess there was a shortage of desperate college elves this year.

Being an elf again would be a definite step backward.

"Oh, and I was talking to your uncle Donny today, and he said you can borrow his pickup truck. He bought a new one. He was going to give it to your cousin Luke, but he wanted a car instead."

"Yeah, a car that doesn't reek like wet dog, manure, and tobacco." I about gagged at the thought of the truck my cousin Luke and I used to drive around my uncle's field, picking pumpkins.

Nothing like adding salt to the wound of my repoed car.

"At least it's a vehicle. You can use my car most evenings and weekends to get to your elf job, but the truck would be a backup in case I need my car. And you can use it for job hunting and interviews."

That would make a great first impression if I showed up at an interview smelling like I'd been shoveling cow dung.

My phone beeped, signaling another call. Rachel. I thanked Mom and answered the call.

"I left the contract for the step dancers on my desk. I need you to check it and see what time they were scheduled to start. I swear to God if they no-show like that damn temp, I'm going to lose it."

I could cover for a sausage, but no way could I fake my way through a step dance.

I'd made it almost the entire day without Rachel noticing my leprechaun socks, or asking to run out shopping because I'd forgotten half my suitcase. I wasn't admitting anything now.

"Sure. I'm in the bathroom. I'll call you back."

Crap. I grabbed a size eight black pair of undies, praying they would fit. I'd have to sneak out again to find a cheaper store. The black socks only cost four bucks, so I splurged and bought five pairs. They were cotton socks, thicker than my leprechaun socks, so hopefully they'd help my shoes stay on. At least I'd *look* professional, even if I didn't *feel* professional.

I stepped outside into a steady mist, and a cool breeze sent a shiver up my back. It hadn't looked like rain when I'd left the hotel. I realized I'd also forgotten to pack an umbrella. Ireland's rain and humidity were wreaking havoc on my naturally wavy hair, and I wouldn't have time to flat-iron it.

So much for looking professional.

CHAPTER SEVEN

Shrouded in a light mist, Malahide Castle had stood stoically for over eight hundred years, persevering against Ireland's harsh climate and likely dozens of invasions. Not only was this my first castle but the oldest building I'd ever visited.

I asked Declan to snap a few quick pics of me in front of the castle as we escorted the group up the gravel path. "Make sure you get all the ivy and those windows." Green and red vines softened the castle's stone exterior. Crisscross grids, resembling pieces of lace, adorned the tall windows.

"Right, then. So you'd also like the castle in the photo, would ya?"

I smiled. "You know what I mean."

A breeze blew a few stray wisps of hair across my face, and I blinked away the raindrops on my eyelashes, trying to keep my eyes open while Declan snapped a few shots, my waterproof mascara being put to the test. I was going to have to Photoshop my hair in all my Ireland pics.

"Do you think we'll be able to take a tour?" I asked.

"Would imagine so," Declan said.

"You've seen one castle, you've pretty much seen them all." Gretchen strutted alongside Declan, tossing her blond hair over her shoulder.

Declan shook his head, disagreeing. "Ireland's castles are modest compared to the likes of Windsor or Neuschwanstein."

I made a mental note to Google both and added them to my bucket list of castles to visit.

"What castles have you been to?" Gretchen asked me.

Cinderella's Castle at Disney World.

"This is my first," I reluctantly admitted.

"Really?" She acted surprised, when she'd undoubtedly assumed I'd never seen a castle, or she wouldn't have asked.

"I remember my first castle," Declan said. "My grandparents took me to Blarney. I kissed the Blarney stone, and then my mates told me the workers and locals pissed on it for craic."

My top lip curled back. "Seriously?"

He shrugged. "When you're a young lad, you believe anything." He slowed his pace, gesturing toward the castle. "Savor this moment. You won't ever see your first castle again. And this job will eventually make you cynical. Nothing will wow you. A four-star hotel becomes slumming it." He smiled. "I envy you."

Gretchen looked at him like he was nuts for envying me.

For once, I actually agreed with her.

I paused, taking a mental picture of the large stone building's round corner towers, red arched door, green and red ivy... I let out a contented sigh. No matter how many castles I might see in my life, I would never forget my first.

Rachel greeted the group at the entrance with a bright smile despite the stress lines around her eyes. The step dancers had arrived later than contracted, so they wouldn't be performing when we entered. I handed Rachel the contract as she escorted us up a red-carpeted, winding staircase and through a room paneled in wood so dark it was almost black. The connecting room was bright and airy with paintings of the castle's previous residents filling the cream-colored walls. Golden chandeliers hung over the two wooden banquet tables with ornate candelabras running down the centers. The taper candles' flames danced to the soft Celtic background music. Waiters in black tuxes served Flanagan's and Brecker Dark in crystal beer glasses, and Kildare Sausage cocktail weenies in puff pastries.

Ten minutes later, three teenaged girls, wearing brightly colored dresses with elaborate designs and detailing, greeted the Kildare Sausage and Flanagan's executives with a lively dance on a narrow balcony at the front of the room. Their heels clicked against the wooden floor, their blond ringlet wigs bouncing in rhythm to the Irish tune. Once everyone was seated, Rachel led our staff to the dark room and assigned our roles for the evening. Mine was to stand in the entrance foyer, directing people to the bathrooms and outside to smoke. Signs pointed down the hall to the bathrooms, and the exit was at the bottom of the stairs from the banquet hall—you couldn't miss either. One little VIP mishap and this was the only position Rachel trusted me with.

The festive music drifted down from the dining hall to the entrance. I held my back ramrod straight, slapped my hands on my hips, and did a little jig, mimicking the dancers. My ankle had stopped throbbing, thanks to four ibuprofen.

My phone rang. Mom. I let it go to voicemail. I texted her that Rachel frowned on personal calls and texts while working. She texted back *Check your e-mail*. Didn't it go without saying that e-mailing was also frowned upon? And I was trying to keep phone usage to a minimum due to the insane cost of international service. The castle didn't offer free Wi-Fi. Of course, my curiosity got the best of me, and I turned toward the wall, discreetly pulling up my e-mail. I immediately regretted it.

While buying gas, Mom had seen a sign that Moto Mart was hiring. How perfect was that? Her words, not mine. If I didn't want to use Uncle Donny's pickup, I'd need a job within walking distance, and it would be full time, not temporary like the elf job. A job application was attached. I did a mental eye roll, but I should appreciate her efforts. I hadn't thought she'd ever play headhunter for me again. She'd landed me my last job thanks to her friend Patsy. She'd been upset about me being fired, so I'd had to confide in her about my ex's obsessive and psycho behavior without going into detail about his emotional abuse. Unlike Rachel, Mom hadn't seen past his deceivingly charismatic facade.

Visions of me in a pea-green Moto Mart polo shirt, pumping bitchy former classmate Megan Fischer's gas, flashed through my mind. It would be my luck she'd be home visiting from New York so she could rub her successful magazine career in my face. No way was I working at Moto Mart. But without a car or Uncle Donny's pickup, I couldn't look for work or *get* to work if I landed a job.

Or rather *when* I landed a job.

"When do the buses head back?" a man asked, causing me to jump.

I spun around to find Rachel's spy. What was with this guy always wanting to leave?

"After dinner and the tours," I said.

His gaze narrowed. "But about what time?"

I have no clue. You do the math.

Of course I couldn't say that or admit I didn't know, so I lied. "Nine o'clock." I hoped that was close to the actual time. He bought it and headed outside, phone in hand.

Tom Reynolds walked down the stairs from the hall, dressed in tan slacks and a blue-and-tan plaid oxford shirt. My gaze darted around the tiny foyer. Nowhere to hide. Perhaps I exuded more confidence and professionalism in my new black socks. The thicker socks were helping my shoes stay on, preventing another tripping incident.

Hopefully, I could answer his questions.

"How are things going?" he asked.

"Fine," I lied. "Are you having a good time?"

"It's Ireland. How can you not?"

If you were dressed like a sausage or had tripped in front of the company's CEO...

"We haven't been formerly introduced. You've been

helping me, and I don't even know your name." He held out his hand. "Tom Reynolds."

As if I didn't know who he was.

I shook his hand. "Caity Shaw."

He arched a brow with interest. "Are you Rachel's sister?"

I nodded, surprised he hadn't known. Yet it wasn't like Rachel made idle chitchat with the CEO.

"I see the resemblance now."

Rachel and I had the same blue eyes, our only similarity, physically or otherwise.

A woman walked down the stairs, and he slipped an arm around her shoulders, drawing her against him. "And this lovely lady is my wife, Kathleen."

Kathleen was much shorter than her husband and at least ten years younger. Her long brown hair was pulled back in a loose twist, and minimal makeup enhanced her natural beauty. She wore a brown tweed pencil skirt, a cream sweater, brown scarf, and brown leather boots. It resembled an outfit Catherine, Duchess of Cambridge, would wear to an English polo match. I had to admit, I'd recorded Kate and William's wedding and had several collector-edition magazines documenting their lives from childhood.

I smiled and introduced myself.

"My dad used to call me Katydid." Her face lit up at the fond memory.

Rachel walked down the stairs, joining us.

"I didn't realize Caity's your sister," Tom said.

Rachel's bright smile camouflaged the fleeting look of panic and hesitation in her eyes. Her cheeks turned a faint pink. "Um, yes, she is."

Had she momentarily entertained the thought of denying our relationship? I'd seen Rachel look frustrated, angry, displeased, exasperated, and annoyed at me. But this was a new one.

Rachel looked embarrassed to admit we were sisters.

Tom smiled. "We're certainly in good hands this meeting, with two Shaw ladies."

I plastered on my best perky smile, attempting to brush aside my hurt feelings and the lump of emotion lodged in my throat. After finding out the CEO had peeled me off the pavement this morning, Rachel undoubtedly hadn't planned to disclose we were sisters. I didn't want him to know our relationship either. This put a ton more pressure on me to not screw up. Rachel was an event-planning goddess. What if Tom Reynolds now expected this same level of professionalism and experience from me, despite my tripping mishap? What if Rachel wasn't around and he turned to me for assistance? I could never be alone with Tom Reynolds again. Ever. Rachel's reputation was at stake. Not to mention, she wouldn't hire me for her local meeting in two weeks if I screwed up.

Here I'd thought being a human arrow directing people would be a no-brainer.

Tom and his wife headed toward the bathrooms.

Rachel turned to me, her forehead wrinkled with concern. "Did Tom need something?"

"No, just asking how I liked Ireland."

Her gaze narrowed further. "You're sure he was okay?"

"Yes. I'm sure." Was she going to drill me now every time I talked to Tom?

Rachel's features relaxed slightly. "Okay. Remember, you need to tell me anything that happens so I'm not blindsided."

Her confidence in me was underwhelming. I brushed aside my frustration and nodded reassuringly. "I will."

"Everyone will be off on tours soon, so you guys can eat. Make sure you take a tour. It's supposed to be one of the best castles in Ireland."

"How many castles have you been to here?"

"This is my first."

"How many have you been to in the world?"

Her gaze narrowed in contemplation. "Not sure. Maybe a dozen."

I couldn't imagine not knowing the exact number of castles I'd visited. Guess that was what Declan meant by no longer being wowed. No worries about that happening to me.

Rachel slipped an energy drink from her purse and discreetly slammed it before heading back up to the dining hall.

No wonder Tom hadn't realized we were related. Even when we were alone, Rachel maintained a professional, distant attitude toward me rather than a warm, familial one. I tried not to think about her reaction to Tom discovering we were sisters, assuring myself I'd misread her look. That we hadn't grown even further apart than I'd feared. We didn't spend nearly the time together that we once did. I was rusty when it came to interpreting Rachel's emotions.

That had to be it.

But I knew it wasn't.

I never wanted to see that look on her face again. I'd always been proud of Rachel. Her career, travels, ambition, and determination. It hurt that she didn't feel the same pride toward me. She'd think even less of me if I told her how I'd allowed my ex to treat me.

After the tours kicked off, I went to grab a bite to eat.

"It's lukewarm," Gretchen said. "I'm going to skip it and go find Rachel." She strutted off.

Thank God. I'd rather eat alone.

A waiter seated me in a high-back wooden chair, and I stared down the long, empty table at the flickering candles. I glanced around at the portraits on the walls, envisioning the previous residents joining me for dinner to discuss the menu for an upcoming ball or what flowers to plant in the castle's twenty-two-acre garden.

The waiter returned with a china plate displaying a work of art. A filet smothered in gravy made with Flanagan's beer, salmon drizzled in dill sauce, and Kildare Sausages on a bed of mashed potatoes—called bangers and mash. I snapped a pic of the fancy meal. I merely sampled each entrée, not wanting to waste time eating when there was so much to see.

Declan walked in during a conversation with my imaginary friends and quirked a curious brow.

"Thought sausages weren't called bangers here?" I said.

He laughed. "We're a complicated lot, we Irish. If it's an English dish, they're bangers. So dining with the castle's ghosts, are ya? Have you met The

White Lady?" He sat down, relaxing back in the chair.

I shook my head, glancing around.

"The painting of a beautiful woman in a long white dress hung here in the Great Hall for years, her identity unknown. When the last Talbot family member, Rose, sold the castle in the 1970s, she took the painting with her to the family home in Tasmania. The woman's spirit has wandered the halls here ever since, in search of the painting."

Declan told the story in a mysterious manner, like you'd do at a slumber party with a flashlight shining up at your face. A chill slithered up my back, and the hairs on my arms stood up. I glanced around, expecting to see an apparition in a flowing white dress.

"A lost soul," I muttered. "Trying to figure out where she belonged." I could relate.

"A shame you won't be here for the castle's haunted Halloween tour."

"You celebrate Halloween in Ireland?"

"Celebrate it? We started it two thousand years ago with the Samhain festival."

"Did you trick-or-treat when you were little?"

"One year I dressed up like Buzz Lightyear from *Toy Story*, and my younger sister, Zoe, went as Jessie. I was going through my astronaut phase."

"Are you two close?"

"Not as close as we once were." He shrugged off a look of regret. "That's the way it goes."

I nodded in understanding. "One year I went as Catwoman, and Rachel went as Batman. My mom said a little girl couldn't go as Batman. Rachel threw a fit, insisting that was sexual discrimination. That a girl could be anything a man could be. My mom said yeah, except for a man."

Declan laughed. "So your mum let her go as Batman, did she?"

"Yeah, there was no arguing with Rachel."

Declan and I were in the middle of eating, when an older lady entered the room. "Would you be wanting to join the last tour?"

"Absolutely." I popped up from my chair.

Declan joined me, even though he'd likely taken the tour so often he could conduct it. The guide led us into the dark wood-paneled room and gestured to a section on the wall. "Behind there is the priest's hole, a hiding place created to conceal priests during a time when Catholics were persecuted under English rule. Priest holes were specially disguised within a house to hide from search parties."

"Too bad I hadn't known about it earlier when I was trying to avoid Tom."

"What happened?" Declan asked.

I shook my head. "Nothing."

"I'm sure it was a bigger deal to you than it was to him."

It'd been the biggest deal to Rachel. The look on her face still haunted me more than any castle ghost.

The tour guide led us into an orangish-peach room, where we joined a group of our attendees. I snapped pics of gilded framed paintings, ornate crystal chandeliers, antique furnishings, and large marble fireplaces. I felt as overwhelmed and awed as Elizabeth Bennett had on her first visit to Darcy's Pemberley estate.

"This is a courting couch." The guide gestured to a cream-colored couch with decorative wood trim. "The couple would sit on it while their chaperone sat on the seat at the end."

I had my picture taken by the couch. "I better not show my mom this pic, or she'll buy one of these couches. After my ex, she's going to want to approve my boyfriends."

A curious smile curled the corners of Declan's mouth. Panic raced through me. What if he questioned me about my ex? I quickly commented on the intricately carved birds in the ceiling's crown molding and moved on to the next room.

I snapped over a hundred pics on the tour. Afterward, we headed outside, and I took a dozen more as we explored the castle's exterior, illuminated with lights and well-lit paths. We walked past a stone abbey missing its windows and roof, surrounded by a cemetery with gravestones and Celtic crosses.

"Omigod, I can't imagine my family being buried in our backyard. Well, except our cat Izzy and hamster Bruno are buried there. But that's different. This is kind of creepy."

We stopped in the souvenir shop, where I browsed through postcards.

"I used to send my granny a postcard from everywhere I went." Declan frowned. "When she died last year, she had almost eighty cards. I kept them."

"How sweet," I said.

Mom would now have *one*.

"The last card I sent her was from Prague. She died while I was there." Regret filled his eyes. "Sometimes you have to believe there's something more after death. It's the only thing that helps you live with a loss." He walked away.

Wow, kind of profound for Declan.

Was that why he hadn't been home in a while? Mourning his grandma's death? No, his friend at the pub had mentioned it'd been a few years since whatever had happened.

I snagged a postcard, planning to send it to my friend Ashley as a peace offering. We hadn't spoken in over a year. Since she'd called my ex an arrogant ass and I'd insisted she was merely jealous I'd landed a gorgeous older guy with money and a prestigious job.

Again, this showed how brainwashed I'd been, sounding like my ex's narcissistic personality disorder had been contagious.

CHAPTER EIGHT

I returned to my room to find a massive gift basket on my desk. The card read *Enjoy a Taste of Ireland*. Sláinte! *Tom Reynolds & Brecker*. Except for disclosing my identity to the CEO, and Rachel's embarrassed reaction over his discovery, the evening had been one of the best ever. Having merely sampled dinner, I was starving. I unwrapped the basket and uncorked the red wine, toasting a wonderful evening. I ate a piece of Irish whiskey fudge, a Baileys truffle, and a chunk of the Irish cream chocolate bar. Afraid I was going to become wasted off of candy, I opened a box of shamrock-shaped shortbread cookies made of pure butter. Deciding I needed to save the rest for missed meals, I pushed the basket aside.

Still on an adrenaline high over visiting my first castle, and now an added sugar rush, I wasn't the least bit tired and decided to update my travel journal. I glossed over the first two days, noting I'd been too crazy busy to write, but had gone to my first Irish pub and drank my first Guinness. I wrote a detailed description of my first castle. Like Declan said, I needed to savor my firsts. However, I still didn't document my first time playing a sausage.

I booted up my laptop. No e-mail offering me the executive admin job. However, Mom's e-mail with the Moto Mart application popped up, as well as one from the temp agency about the elf job. For a few glorious hours, I'd actually been able to forget about my pathetic job prospects and repoed car. I wanted desperately to delete both e-mails. But what if I didn't have a full-time job soon?

I found my car insurance card in my wallet and e-mailed the agent to cancel my policy. Insurance on my sporty car was outrageous. Hopefully, the refund paid off one of my department store credit cards, enabling me to close out my first account.

After locking the door, I once again barricaded it with the desk chair, my suitcase, and the rest of my makeshift security system. I put on my jammies and slipped on the white velvet robe. I grabbed my cell phone and relaxed back on the red upholstered settee. Mom had left me a voicemail when I was on the bus back from the castle. If I didn't return her call, she'd forget the time difference and call me at three in the morning. In desperate need of sleep, I didn't want her or hotel security waking me up in the middle of the night. I speed dialed her, planning on keeping it brief so it didn't cost me a half-day's pay.

"Did you get the Moto Mart application?" she asked.

"Yeah, uh, thanks."

"You better not wait until you're home to submit it.

Jobs in town are scarce, so they go fast. Patsy's son Tyler handed in an application."

Tyler was a high school dropout who'd lost his license after parking his parents' car in the middle of a street in a drunken stupor. It'd be my luck I'd submit an application and he'd land the job instead of me.

"I know the job isn't ideal, but at least you'd have a stable income until you can find a better one, which you will. With your college degree, you'll find a great job."

Where were these high expectations while I was growing up?

"Everything going okay with Rachel?"

"Yeah, fine. Ireland is wonderful."

"I wish I could have gone there with my mother, her being Irish and all. She never talked about Ireland or showed any interest in returning there."

I perked up. "Grandma Brunetti was *born* in Ireland? I thought her ancestors came over, like, years ago during the famine." I'd only been seven when she'd died, so I vaguely remembered her. "She didn't have an Irish accent, did she?"

"She tried hard to hide it. But I must have mentioned at some point she came from Ireland."

If Mom had, I couldn't recall. While growing up, I wouldn't have been interested in the heritage of a grandma I'd barely known. When you were young, you cared about the present and future more than the past.

"Her family name was Coffey. They were from County Westmeath. Don't think I ever knew the town. She was always very secretive about her life in Ireland."

It didn't surprise me that Mom knew little about her

mother's background. They'd never been close, from what I'd gathered. Mom rarely mentioned her. Maybe that was why Mom was a bit overbearing. She hoped we'd have a closer relationship than she'd had with her mom.

"She claimed she left Ireland because her family was all dead. Yet after her death, we found letters her older sister Theresa had written to her over the years, along with a letter from Theresa's daughter after she died, a few years before my mother. The letters were dated, but no envelopes, so we didn't know where her sister had lived or her married name."

My family got on my nerves, but I couldn't imagine not seeing Rachel for fifty years and not attending her funeral. I feared that might happen if we didn't reconnect on this trip. Friends came and went, but I'd always believed that family would be there for me.

Right now, I wasn't so sure.

"So her entire family stayed in Ireland?"

"As far as I know."

"Why did she come to the US if her family wasn't actually dead?"

"I always assumed she had a falling out with them. Why lie about them being dead if she liked them?" Mom's tone grew bitter, and I could picture her lips pressed into a thin line. "But she seemed to have liked her sister Theresa. Especially since she named my sister Teri after her, which of course we never knew until after my mother died."

"Maybe they were all dead except her sister."

"No, one of the letters mentioned her mother's death when I would have been a teenager. That was just like my mother, keeping secrets and never being open with us. I'm sure she'd have gotten rid of the letters if she'd known she was going to have a heart attack. She wouldn't have wanted us to find them. Dottie and I wanted to throw the letters away after we read them, but Teri insisted on keeping them, being named after our aunt who wrote them. I would guess she still has them, along with my mother's naturalization papers, which might note the town she grew up in. Maybe you're close enough you could drive out and visit it."

I barely had time to pee during this program, let alone time to pop over to my ancestors' homeland. Even though the idea intrigued me.

"I'm sorry I never told you all of this. I guess it was too difficult to talk about. It really hurt that she lied to us for so many years, and made me angry that we couldn't confront her when we found the letters."

"I'm sorry I never asked about her."

I felt horrible that I'd never showed interest in Grandma. She might have been a distant, closed-off mother, but she'd also been a brave woman, moving across the ocean to a strange, unknown land by herself. Why had she left Ireland? Had she been stalked by an ex? Her family had been IRA bombers, wanted by the law? Too bad I hadn't inherited Grandma's courage and sense of adventure. I eyed the chair, suitcase, and other items blocking the door.

I could really use both about now.

CHAPTER
NINE

The next morning, I didn't have to start work until seven, so I washed all of my hair, not merely my bangs, and flat-ironed it. Even though the moment I stepped outside it would be a frizzy mess, there was a good chance I wouldn't see the light of day. I did my full makeup routine, including foundation. The hotel provided a coffeemaker with an assortment of teas and coffee. I made a cup of tea while waiting for the iron to heat up. I took a sip of the hot golden-colored beverage, happy to discover it was the same tea I'd drank at breakfast yesterday. I ironed my clothes, then reluctantly slipped off the hotel's velvet robe, got dressed, and put in some black chandelier earrings.

I headed to the office fifteen minutes early, with a zip in my step, still on a high over visiting my first castle. And Declan was right. I might get the hang of this job. Even though I'd only been a bathroom and smoking attendant, I hadn't directed anyone down into the dungeon by mistake. And I'd convinced myself that

Tom Reynolds had indulged in a few whiskeys and didn't even recall I was Rachel's sister. And that Rachel hadn't actually looked like she'd wanted to *forget* we were sisters. I had to get over it. Instead, I focused on our Irish grandma and how anxious I was to share my discovery with Rachel, to remind her that we were family, not merely coworkers.

I walked into the office, and my zip was zapped.

Gretchen and Rachel sat in front of Rachel's computer, chatting over coffee, like best buds. So much for some sisterly bonding time. I plastered on a bright smile.

"Rachel's showing me pictures of her new condo. Well, I guess it isn't new. You've been there almost a year. It's gorgeous."

I nodded, even though I'd never seen pictures of it or been there. I peered over Gretchen's shoulder at the digital photos. Copper pots and pans hung from a rack over a large island in the kitchen. Since when did Rachel cook?

"Thanks. It's nice, but really small." Rachel closed out of the photos, looking a bit uncomfortable showing off her condo when I lived in my old bedroom with the same pink walls and pink lacy comforter. "I'm glad you're down early, Caity. Did you receive a gift basket in your room?" She gestured to the basket on Gretchen's desk, identical to the one I'd raided last night before going to bed. I nodded, and luckily, before I could thank her, she said, "Can you go get it? The hotel screwed up and delivered them to the staff rooms."

My stomach took a swan dive.

"The vendor dropped the baskets off at the bellstand, and I provided a rooming list with our names crossed off, but one of the bellmen spilled tea on it, ran a new list, and never crossed us off. They ended up four baskets short." She glanced over at Gretchen. "And of course, you-know-who didn't receive one, so I want to deliver them before she calls me."

Declan walked in carrying his gift basket. "I'm guessing I wasn't supposed to get this?"

"Thanks. Set it next to Gretchen's."

Maybe the hotel sold the same wine, since it was produced locally. Yeah, for a gazillion euros. I could possibly repackage some of the snacks... I didn't have money to replace an entire basket! How was I supposed to know we didn't get the baskets? Even though everyone else had figured it out. I had no choice but to tell Rachel. She could probably still smell the Baileys truffle on my breath I'd eaten before coming down. But I refused to admit my ignorance in front of Declan and Gretchen.

"You can run up and grab the basket after our team meeting," Rachel said. "It'll be quick. Today's going to be easy. Most of the group is going to the Kildare Sausage plant. I'll have you load the bus, Declan, and then head over there for the return. Caity, I'll have you see off the wives' walking tour and shadow Gretchen."

I almost threw up my Baileys truffle.

"Gretchen has been doing this job as long as me. She can give you some great training."

Gretchen smiled sweetly. "I'd be happy to. The BEOs are on my desk."

I walked over and scanned her desk, no clue what a BEO was.

"Oh, sorry. A BEO is a Banquet Event Order. On the left there. But you know what? We can go over those later. I need you to arrange an in-room massage for ten o'clock, and she prefers a male masseuse. The spa opens in a half hour. Pop by there rather than calling. Doing it in person last minute is always a good idea. And she's going to wig out if they can't fit her in."

Great. So if this woman couldn't get an appointment, it was my fault.

Gretchen scribbled a room number and name on a sticky note. She answered her ringing cell phone and walked out for better service. Declan left to work breakfast, and I went over to Rachel and confessed about the basket and apologized.

Rachel's jaw tightened, but she shrugged it off. "It's not your fault. You didn't know."

Yeah, but Gretchen and Declan had known.

"What snacks do you think need to be replaced?"

"Ah...probably the whiskey fudge, the Irish cream chocolate, and the cookies. Oh, and I opened the wine." I could probably retie the bow on the individually wrapped Baileys truffles. "I'll pay for everything."

She raised a questioning brow, like how the hell had I eaten all of that in such a short period of time? "Don't worry about the money. The hotel will pick up the bill. It was their screwup. Just so you know, staff never receives two-hundred-dollar gift baskets or top-end amenities. If we're handing out T-shirts or duffel bags, that's different."

That gift basket had cost two hundred freakin' dollars?

Desperate to change the subject, I said, "I talked to Mom last night, and she mentioned Grandma Brunetti came from Ireland. Did you know that?" Rachel was five years older than me, so she probably had more vivid memories of Grandma. All I could remember was her house had smelled like garlic, she had cute little teacups lined up on her windowsills, and all her walls were yellow.

Rachel's gaze narrowed. "I knew she was Irish. I didn't know she'd actually come from Ireland."

"Remember how she'd serve us hot chocolate in those little floral teacups and let us wear her aprons? I always wore her purple apron, and you wore the yellow one with sunflowers. So it worked out well."

Rachel nodded, smiling, relaxing back in her chair for the first time since we'd arrived in Dublin. Her reaction gave me a sense of hope that she had fond childhood memories of us, not merely bad ones, like all her feetless Barbies.

"She made the best Irish brown bread, smeared with homemade blackberry jam," Rachel said. "Of course, I didn't know it was Irish bread back then. We each got a teacup after she died, but I don't know if I've seen mine since I moved." She brushed a contemplative finger lightly over her red lips.

My teacup sat on my bedroom dresser.

"Too bad Mom never made that bread," I said. "She hates baking, and she and Grandma weren't that close, so she probably didn't want to carry on the family traditions. Kind of sad. I wish I could remember her better. She was from County Westmeath, but Mom doesn't know the town. Grandma never talked about Ireland." I recounted Mom's story about finding her aunt's letters after believing her mom's entire family had been dead. "Teri has the letters and Grandma's naturalization papers. Mom's going to ask her if either mention the town she was from and—"

"Powerscourt just called about the dinner," Gretchen said, flying into the room, phone in hand. "I'm not sure how you're going to feel about the menu change. Do you have a sec?"

"Sure, I'm not in the middle of anything."

Except for discussing our childhood memories and family history. Granted, we were working, but couldn't a dinner later in the week wait two minutes? Rachel went over to powwow with Gretchen without excusing herself or promising that we'd chat more about Grandma later. They stepped out of the office.

I seethed with frustration!

Declan strolled in.

"Where'd you grow up?" I asked.

"County Meath, in the Midlands."

"Our grandma came from Westmeath."

"That's next to Meath. What town was your granny from?"

"Not sure. My mom's going to get back to me."

"When was she born?"

"My mom's fifty-eight..." I twisted my mouth in contemplation. "And I remember her saying my grandma was almost forty when she was born, so I'd guess my grandma was born 1920ish."

"The 1911 census and other records are online. I helped my granny research her dad's line. You might be able to find her family. What was her name?"

"Bridget Coffey."

"Ah, a lovely Irish name. What were her parents' names?"

I shrugged. "I'll have to ask my mom if she knows."

Declan didn't appear to judge me for knowing so little about Grandma, when he'd sent his grandma postcards from around the world. However, *I* was judging me.

"She died when I was only seven." I attempted to justify my ignorance.

"Since she wasn't born yet in the 1911 census, the town and any names would help us find her family."

"I know she had an older sister Theresa."

I promptly e-mailed Mom, requesting Grandma's birth year and family members' names, if she knew any besides Theresa.

I went to my room to salvage what I could of the gift basket and popped some ibuprofen. I reassembled the basket without the wine and the open food items. At least I'd have snacks if I missed a meal. I was about to walk out the door, and realized I'd left the spa sticky note on the desk. Afraid I'd misplace it, and God forbid have to ask Gretchen for the info again, I typed the room number and name, which looked like Winston, into my phone and tossed the note.

I ran the basket down to the office. Thankfully, Rachel was the only one there. I apologized again. I headed to the spa and waited outside for it to open. I eyed my unpolished nails and ragged cuticles. No longer able to afford regular manicures, I needed to at least start polishing them. I'd totally let myself go over the past few months.

The spa opened, and I stepped inside. A soothing lavender and vanilla scent greeted me, along with a blond receptionist in a seafoam-green dress. I inhaled a deep breath, my shoulders relaxing, a serene feeling washing over me.

She confirmed a ten o'clock appointment. I took one last deep breath, not wanting to leave. The woman informed me the scent could be mine in the form of a candle or spray for a mere twenty-five euros. I'd pop by and stick my head in the door whenever I needed a *free* fix. Which would be every five minutes for as long as I was stuck shadowing Gretchen.

I went down to breakfast to share the great news with Gretchen.

"Perfect," she said. "I'll give her a call and let her know."

If I hadn't been able to secure an appointment, I would have undoubtedly been the one passing along the bad news.

"Be outside her room fifteen minutes prior to make sure the masseuse shows up, but don't let him knock until ten. Throws off her Zen if he's early. And don't stay when he knocks—that's awkward."

The masseuse arrived ten minutes early, so I had him wait and knock as scheduled, then I bolted. Fifteen minutes later, the office phone rang.

Rachel answered it. As she listened to the caller, her eyes widened with panic. "So sorry. Let me get right on that." She hung up, and her gaze darted to me. "I thought you said Lindsey's masseuse showed up at her room?"

"He did. Fifteen minutes ago."

"That was her. He's still not there."

"No way. I was standing right by her door, room 1024."

"Room 1042." Gretchen's jaw tightened. Her green eyes darkened.

I opened my cell phone's note app. "1024."

"You must have typed it in wrong," Gretchen snapped.

"No...I didn't," I said hesitantly. Had I? No, no way, I'd doubled-checked her note. Hadn't I? Yes!

I was right.

I was strong.

I was worthy.

Martha's mantra.

"Did you reconfirm her name with the spa?" Rachel asked.

"I wasn't sure what the name was. I couldn't read it."

Gretchen rolled her eyes, like I was full of it.

Rachel phoned the spa and hung up after a brief conversation. "They said they tried calling the cell number you provided."

I glanced down at my phone. One new message. "I must have been in a dead zone. I don't know why my phone didn't signal a voicemail. Can he run up to her room now?"

"She leaves on a tour in an hour."

"I'm sorry, but I swear I didn't screw up."

Rachel looked skeptical, like she was once again

mentally counting to ten. "Don't worry about it. Nothing we can do now."

I *would* worry about it.

And now I'd be too embarrassed to pop into the spa for my aromatherapy fix. Which I desperately needed!

I bolted up to my room to fish the note out of the garbage. My bed had been made, my garbage emptied. I flew out the door, zoning in on the maid cart at the end of the hall. I ran down and knocked on the open guest-room door. The maid poked her head out—an older woman with a pleasant smile in a beige dress with a white apron.

"Did you clean room 1530?"

Her forehead crinkled in confusion, and she responded in German or some Eastern European language. I hadn't known where Budapest was located on a map until two days ago. I certainly couldn't determine if someone was speaking Hungarian versus Romanian. I grabbed a pad of paper and a pen off her cart and jotted down my room number and pointed down the hallway. She nodded in understanding. I gestured at the garbage bags and then myself, wanting to determine which bag held mine. She pointed to one, and I snatched it off the cart. She took a step back, looking a bit freaked out. I dropped down onto the floor. Garbage flew onto the red plush carpeting as I plowed through the bag.

"Is everything okay?" a man asked.

I peered up to find Tom Reynolds and another VIP watching me with curiosity. Seriously? What was the chance of running into Tom Reynolds while digging through the garbage? So much for my plan to avoid the

CEO. Another VIP walked out of a room behind me, holding a sparkling water. A sign next to the door read *Concierge Lounge.* Rachel had mentioned our group had access to the lounge, which offered free snacks and beverages, but I hadn't realized it was on my floor. Not like I'd had free time to hang out there.

"Yeah, just accidentally threw away…something."

They walked off, Tom glancing back at me sitting there up to my *knickers* in garbage. Hopefully, he didn't mention the humiliating incident in front of Rachel, inquiring if I ever found my lost item in the garbage. But what if he did? Rachel had insisted I tell her about every interaction I had with the CEO. This wasn't as mortifying as my tripping incident but ran a close second. After Rachel's embarrassed look of me at the castle, no way was I telling her about this.

I finally found the sticky note, confirming I hadn't screwed up. Still, my chest tightened. Gretchen was going to make my life a living hell. I knew I was right—maybe that was all that mattered… No way. It mattered that Rachel knew I hadn't effed up. I'd see Rachel the rest of my life, and I prayed to God I never saw Gretchen again.

I went down to the office and showed Rachel the note.

Gretchen gave me the evil eye, her gaze softening when she peered over at Rachel. "I'm so sorry, Rachel."

Rachel shrugged it off, looking surprised that her precious Gretchen had messed up rather than me. "These things happen. I think you're allowed one screwup every five years."

What the hell? I'd obviously exceeded my limit of

screwups for five years. Or rather my *life*, as far as Rachel was concerned. She didn't believe I could do this job. Hell, she didn't believe I could do *any* job. And Mom thought I should settle for being an elf!

Well, I could do this job, and I was going to prove it.

Or die trying, as Declan had said!

Chapter Ten

Women trickled down to the hotel lobby for the walking tour, but I had yet to see Anna, the tour guide. I needed to confirm that she knew the restaurant had changed. She finally arrived ten minutes prior to the tour's departure, with the correct walking map but not the updated restaurant.

"Are you sure it was switched to Paddy's Pub?" she asked.

Declan was walking through the lobby and made a detour toward us. "Is something wrong?"

"I had Cafferty's for lunch," Anna said.

"No, it's Paddy's," Declan said.

I held up the agenda in my hand. "I have the info right—"

"That's okay. I've got it." Declan cut me off and escorted Anna to the side for a private discussion.

I stood there smiling at the women like an idiot while seething on the inside, trembling with anger. Declan reminded me of my ex, stepping in and taking control of a situation as if I was incapable of handling it. Even worse, my ex had made *me* believe I was incapable of handling it!

And like Rachel, Declan didn't believe I could do this job!

"You lovely ladies ready for some sightseeing?" Declan asked, joining us.

The ladies nodded, a few flashing flirtatious smiles at the charming Declan. I glared at him, my jaw tightening, my heart thumping wildly in my chest.

The tour departed, and Declan turned to me, smiling.

I squared my shoulders. "You just made me look like a total idiot. I had all the info on the new restaurant. I'm capable of giving a tour guide direction. Just because I fell in front of the CEO doesn't mean I'm completely incompetent. So back off."

Declan's gaze narrowed, and he looked freaked out by my tangent. "Sorry. I thought I'd—"

"Step in and take over? Take control? You can really be an ass." I stormed off.

∾❧ ❧∾

I sat in a corner booth of the hotel's pub, perusing the lunch menu. A song about a pretty little girl from Omagh was playing, and more people were entering from the street than the hotel. It appeared to be a popular lunch spot with the locals, so the food should be good. The one day I actually had time for lunch, I wasn't the least bit hungry after all the upset this morning. A young guy in an emerald-green polo with the pub's logo brought me a diet soda, and I ordered my first fish and chips since arriving in Dublin.

I connected to the hotel's Wi-Fi on my iPad so I could surf the web for free. No e-mail from Mom with info on Grandma. It was only 6:00 a.m. at home, or I'd call her, anxious to know if Aunt Teri had Grandma's letters. And still no response from my interview or my thirty-one résumés. However, the insurance agent had replied that my policy expired soon, so I was only receiving a refund of $68.43. That would make a minor dent in my gas card.

I needed to sell my Tiffany diamond stud earrings, a Christmas present from my ex. I was afraid to advertise them online after he'd stalked me on Craigslist. However, a pawnshop had offered me only a quarter of the original cost, which I knew because my ex had bragged about how expensive they were.

I checked employment sites, fairly certain I'd already applied for all the executive admin assistant jobs listed. I had to stop limiting myself to admin positions, my only real work experience. What other jobs was I qualified to do? Honestly, I hadn't really been qualified for my admin job. My organizational and computer skills weren't the best. I was a whiz at word processing programs, but I required an instruction manual for spreadsheet and database software. And being backup for the switchboard operator had sent me into a complete panic. However, I'd enjoyed the few times I'd had to cover for the receptionist, since it got me out of my tiny cubicle and allowed me to interact with people.

Face it. I'd made a better elf than an admin assistant.

I felt someone staring over my shoulder and peered up to find Declan wearing a cautious smile. My body went rigid.

"I hope you aren't looking for a new job because I'm a complete arse." He shifted his stance, fidgeting with the silver Celtic design on the leather band around his wrist.

This was the first time I'd seen Declan lack confidence. My shoulders relaxed slightly. Admitting he was an *arse* earned him a half smile, and maybe I'd overreacted a tad earlier. Pissed over the whole Gretchen spa fiasco, I'd been a volcano waiting to erupt. And I had to stop allowing certain smells, sounds, or people's actions to trigger memories of my ex and provoke such intense emotions. Recognizing the triggers was a step in the right direction. Now I needed to learn to manage, or better yet, prevent them. However, Declan had reminded me of my ex. Not only the way he'd taken control, but his suave and charming demeanor might be a cover for his manipulative behavior. I doubted Declan was like my ex, but I wasn't the best judge of character. I wasn't sure what to think of him.

Knight in shining armor, always coming to my rescue, or controlling ass?

"No, I'm not looking for a new job because you're a jerk, even though you were. I'm only working this meeting to help out Rachel. It's not my new career."

"Right, then. You said that before. Trying to convince yourself, are ya?"

"I hate flying and sleep like crap in hotels. And I need some stability in my life, a full-time job, not one or two meetings a month."

He gestured to the bench across from me.

I nodded fine.

He slipped off his suit jacket and slid into the booth. His white oxford shirt collar and front were crisply pressed, the arms and back a wrinkled mess. He gestured to his shirt. "Why bother ironing more than what people see?"

"I'll have to remember that. Ironing sucks."

"Stick with me—I'll teach you the tricks of the trade."

He glanced down at the menu, then slowly raised his gaze, meeting mine. "Sorry about earlier. I don't think you're incompetent. That wasn't why I stepped in. I'd made the restaurant change and rang the tour company about it, so I knew the situation."

I nodded. I got it, but I was still upset. "Yeah, well, I might have overreacted a tad." However, I was glad I'd stuck up for myself.

"So what job you looking for, then?" he asked.

I had no clue now that I'd decided I really didn't want to be an admin assistant. But I didn't want to admit I had no sense of direction...

"I think I'd like to counsel women."

Where had that come from? I'd been thinking a lot about Martha's advice the past few days. But did I really want to be a counselor?

Caity Shaw—Avenger of Women. Superhero extraordinaire, swooping in and coming to women's rescue with a single business card. That was how it had happened with me. I'd been in a restaurant's bathroom when Martha, the woman at the table next to my ex and me, approached me with a sympathetic smile and a card for the women's shelter and crisis center where she worked. When I assured her my ex wasn't beating me, she pointed out that emotional abuse was as damaging as physical. She'd heard his demeaning comments, such as changing my pasta order to a salad so the new dress he'd bought me for his friend's wedding would fit. He'd always bought me a size too small so I'd have to fast off any extra weight before wearing it. If I couldn't fit into the expensive designer dress, I obviously didn't appreciate it.

Martha had rattled off a slew of other narcissistic personality traits, describing my ex to a tee. She'd had him pegged after eavesdropping for five minutes, whereas I'd been clueless after living with him for two years. She'd left me standing there in the bathroom, dumbfounded yet enlightened.

Ironically, that was the same restaurant my ex had taken me to on our first date. He'd sucked me in, impressing me with an expensive dinner and his charming and attentive manner. He'd even suggested that I have tiramisu for dessert. Once he'd earned my trust, he slowly began to manipulate and control me.

It had taken me several weeks to work up the nerve to call Martha. She'd given me the strength and support to leave my ex.

However, ending the relationship had merely been the first step on my road to recovery. You didn't just rebuild your self-esteem overnight or stop doubting your thoughts, opinions, and ideas when someone had repeatedly questioned and shot them down daily for two years.

"Is that your degree, counseling?"

I glanced up from my diet soda, realizing I'd zoned out. "I majored in sociology."

Because I'd aced a sociology class, the first course that had held my interest, I'd switched my major for the fourth time. Amazingly, it'd only taken me five years to earn my undergrad degree. I couldn't imagine going back for a master's, which many counseling jobs likely required. I'd planned to be a career advisor. I thought helping others find direction in life would help me figure out my own life. I'd applied for the few job openings in the area but never landed an interview. If I'd been sucked in by my ex when I had a sociology degree—the study of human relationships—was I qualified to counsel others?

Although I'd never be fooled again.

"So what made you decide on counseling women?" Declan appeared truly interested in my career aspirations, not merely sucking up after being an ass.

"I know someone who works at a woman's shelter and finds it very fulfilling. I'm going to bring her my hotel toiletries, do what I can to help for now."

If I was too ashamed to tell my sister the truth about my ex, I certainly couldn't confide in someone I barely knew. Besides, Declan was a guy. He might say I'd been overly sensitive to my ex's degrading comments and read too much into them. The same thing I'd told myself until that day in the restaurant when Martha had come to my rescue.

CHAPTER
ELEVEN

After lunch, Declan waited in the lobby for the van to take him to the Kildare Sausage plant to pick up attendees. I wanted to sneak away with him so I didn't have to spend the afternoon shadowing Gretchen. However, sneaking off wouldn't prove I could do this job, not only to Rachel but, more importantly, to myself. I returned to the office, where Rachel and Gretchen were eating salads while glued to their laptops.

I gestured to a small pile of papers on the corner of Gretchen's desk. "Are those the BEOs?"

Gretchen nodded absently without looking up.

I snagged the BEOs. "I'm going to photocopy them since I'm shadowing you this afternoon."

Rachel glanced up, smiling with approval, then buried her face back in her laptop. Gretchen appeared surprised that I still planned on shadowing her after the spa debacle. I wasn't backing down. Next time she snidely drilled me on BEOs, not only would I know what one looked like but what it meant, including her red notes scribbled all over them. I added horrible penmanship to her long list of flaws.

I made copies and placed the originals back on Gretchen's desk. I three-hole-punched the BEOs and added them to my binder, which currently held an attendee list, hotel rooming list, emergency plan, and the meeting agenda. The binder was the same size as Declan's and Gretchen's but with a quarter of the contents. Rather skimpy. What info did they have that I didn't? I needed to fill my binder. Maybe if I *looked* more important, I'd *feel* more important.

I sat down at the desk next to Gretchen's, studying the BEOs. Her red notes detailed things such as alternating the flavors of the jams and juices daily, providing ketchup and hot sauce for the eggs, and a bunch of numbers and abbreviations: GTD, EXP, and ACT. I asked her what these meant.

She stopped typing, forcing a strained smile. She couldn't even fake being nice. Good thing I could.

"Can we go over those later? I have to help Rachel with this other meeting right now."

"Anything I can do, since I'm supposed to be shadowing you?"

"I'll let you know." She continued typing, brushing me off.

I stifled a growl and the urge to scratch her eyes out.

I stared blankly at the unfamiliar acronyms and industry terms and table dimensions given in centimeters, which would have meant little to me in inches. Nice to know we were having French toast for breakfast tomorrow. Now that I was back on carbs, I was tempted to start slipping brown bread in my purse at breakfast to satisfy my late-night cravings.

A Brecker executive walked into the office. He was fortyish, tall, with light-brown hair, and dressed in black slacks and a red Brecker-logoed, button-down shirt. He'd been a witness to my garbage meltdown earlier. Not one of my finer moments. I sprang from my chair, eager to redeem myself and to start a conversation before he could mention the garbage.

"Can I help you?" I asked.

Rachel and Gretchen glanced up from their computers, apparently not having heard him enter the room.

"I can help him," I assured them.

Rachel nodded hesitantly, smiling at the guy, then went back to work, undoubtedly eavesdropping on our conversation. Gretchen was also listening, anxiously waiting for me to screw up.

Distressed lines creased the guy's brow, and his breathing was labored. My heart raced. Great. He had a problem.

"I lost my phone. I thought I left it in my room this morning, but I just checked, and it's not there. I mainly use my work cell, so I didn't even realize my personal one is missing."

I'd misplaced my cell scads of times. I was a pro at locating a lost phone.

"When did you last use it?"

"At the castle last night. I sent my wife pictures of the tour." He rubbed a worried hand over his chin. "All my family pictures are on it, and ones of my dog, Max, who just passed away."

My heart sank over the loss of his dog and all his pics. I had over a thousand pics on my phone. After losing my phone for the third time, I'd finally downloaded them on my computer. I jotted down his name, Martin Brown, and the phone's description. I promised to call his work cell when I located the phone. He thanked me and left, not looking overly hopeful about the phone's recovery.

I felt horrible for the guy. However, I was a bit excited at the prospect of returning to Malahide Castle. Alone. I asked Rachel for her contact at the castle. I called, but no luck. The woman promised to keep an eye out for the phone.

"Maybe he left it on the bus," I said. "I'm going to get Declan's contact for the ground company."

Rachel look mildly impressed that I wasn't asking her for direction on how to resolve the situation. This really wasn't that difficult. Hopefully.

Declan was still in the lobby, waiting on the van to go to the Kildare Sausage plant. I explained the situation.

"No problem at all," he said. "I have the ground's dispatch on speed dial. I'll ring them."

"Would it be okay if I called?" Ground was Declan's gig, and I didn't want to step on his toes after I'd gone berserk over him taking charge of the tour earlier, but I needed to do this on my own.

"That'd be grand. My van just drove in." He gladly gave me the number.

I gestured to the thick stack of ground transportation paperwork on his clipboard. "Can I get a copy of that later?"

He shrugged. "Sure."

The stack of papers would help bulk up my binder.

I called dispatch, and within five minutes the guy had located the lost phone wedged in a seat on last night's bus. The driver was in the area and would drop it off in ten minutes.

Twenty minutes later, I was standing in the lobby, still no driver with a phone. I called the dispatcher back, and he contacted the driver while I held.

He returned to the line. "He said he dropped it off ten minutes ago."

"I've been waiting here twenty, and no driver has been in the lobby. It's dead."

"Hold please." He returned a few minutes later. "The driver dropped it at The River Liffey Hotel."

"I'm not at The River Liffey Hotel. I'm at the Connelly Court Hotel. I'm sure that's the hotel I told you. It's the only one I know in Dublin." There was no way I'd given him the wrong hotel name, which would have been a bigger mistake than if I'd given the spa the wrong room number.

"You did indeed tell me Connelly Court. He dropped a group from the airport earlier at The River Liffey Hotel and had it in his head it was to be dropped there. When he couldn't find you, he left it with the bellstand. I'll have someone run there straight away to collect it and deliver it to you."

"How far is that Liffey hotel from mine?"

"Five blocks."

"I'll go get it."

I wasn't trusting anyone at this point. No way was I telling Rachel they'd delivered it to the wrong hotel.

She'd assume I'd given them the incorrect hotel name, group name, city, or country.

I ran to The River Liffey Hotel, sweating despite the cool fifty-five degrees. An anxiety-induced sweat. Even though I now knew the phone's location, I didn't want Rachel to discover *my* location and that I'd gone off-site without telling her. Sometimes I felt like a prisoner.

Liffey was a totally cute name and a fun word. However, the hotel wasn't so cute with its sparse décor, worn brown furnishings, and dull cream-colored walls.

Declan was right. I was already becoming a hotel snob.

I approached a young guy standing behind the bellstand, dressed in a drab brown uniform. His name badge read *Fintan.* "A bus driver mistakenly dropped a cell phone off a half hour ago. I'm here to pick it up."

Fintan smiled brightly. "We delivered it to the guest's room."

My eyes widened. "How did you deliver it to his room when he's not staying here? I never gave the driver a room number."

"I looked up Mr. Braun's room."

"It's *Brown,* not *Braun.* What's this man's room number?"

Fintan's brow creased in contemplation. "I'm not supposed to give out room numbers."

"You also aren't supposed to deliver a phone to someone who doesn't own it." Okay, that was bitchy. This guy was obviously new and starting to look a bit panicked that his stint at The River Liffey Hotel might be short lived. I could relate. I took a calming breath. "I get how this happened, but can you please give me the room number? If I don't get the phone back, I might lose my job." I was fairly certain that was a fib.

He nodded in understanding, and after debating the dilemma with another bellman, he agreed to escort me to the guest's room. He knocked on the door, and a middle-aged American woman greeted us with a scowl and a curt hello. She didn't look very welcoming, like someone who might not turn over a misdelivered cell phone. The bellman explained the situation.

Her expression relaxed. "I was wondering why my husband had a cell phone I didn't know about."

Thank God her husband wasn't there, or this misunderstanding might have put a serious damper on their vacation.

I called the bus dispatcher to share the good news.

"I'm sorry," he said. "Niall is a very seasoned driver. He must be having an off day."

"That's okay. It happens."

I was starting to think no matter how seasoned you were, shit just happened in this industry. There were too many variables out of your control. You could be a meeting-planning goddess like Rachel, with years of experience, but when you came on-site, it was all about troubleshooting. I wanted to tell Rachel what had happened so she knew how well I'd resolved the issue. However, would she believe I hadn't given dispatch the wrong info, even though I'd proven I hadn't given the wrong room number to the spa?

I was proud of how I'd handled the situation. Maybe being proud of myself was more important than Rachel being proud of me.

CHAPTER
TWELVE

Mr. Brown was ecstatic that I'd found his cell phone. Hopefully, he shared my incredible super-sleuthing skills with Tom Reynolds. Rachel told me "good job," then promptly sent me off on my next task, obtaining additional restaurant options from the concierge in case attendees besides Tom Reynolds stopped by requesting recommendations. After Declan returned from the sausage plant, I copied his paperwork for my binder, now containing almost half the contents of Gretchen's.

What the hell did she have that I still didn't?

My final errand for the day was to pick up office supplies and snacks for the bus tour to County Wicklow later that week. Rachel asked Declan to accompany me under the pretense it would be too much for me to carry. She was probably afraid to have me venture out into a strange city by myself. She didn't know I'd found my way to The River Liffey Hotel, even though it'd only been five blocks.

I popped into the gift shop on my way out and grabbed a bag of cheese-and-onion-flavored Taytos—Ireland's yummy potato chips, or rather *crisps*, as the Irish called them. I didn't want to waste time on dinner. I planned to sneak in some souvenir shopping, and I had to buy undies. Most of the shops closed in two hours. Not that it would take much time to spend my meager souvenir budget. No way were leprechaun socks and shamrock undies going to be my only mementos of my first trip abroad, especially since I'd likely toss the socks, a reminder of my humiliation.

We stepped outside, and I breathed in the fresh air, wanting to yell, *I'm free! I'm free!* No breeze made it feel a bit warmer than earlier, despite dusk settling in. So nice out that Declan only wore jeans and a white T-shirt, which showed off his nicely toned biceps and a tattoo. The tattoo matched the Celtic symbol on his leather bracelet. He was obviously into the design.

Not only did the absence of rain put a bounce in my step but also the absence of Gretchen, who'd stayed at the hotel to help Rachel. Sometimes it paid to be incompetent at your job, like me. Although I wondered if Gretchen felt a bit less competent after her spa screwup. Doubtful. She likely still blamed me. I was proud I'd stuck up for myself.

I reviewed tomorrow's breakfast BEO as we walked down the street, taking advantage of Declan's willingness to share his industry knowledge with me.

"I can't believe a soda costs three times what it does in a store," I said.

"And that doesn't include the service charge, which is generally ten percent here, much higher in the States. I did a meeting in Miami once."

"It says we get a discount on prices."

"Everything is negotiable when you contract a hotel."

I popped the last Tayto into my mouth, peering down the one-way street. Coast clear, I stepped off the curb. Declan grabbed my arm and pulled me back against him as a double-decker bus zoomed past, a blur of yellow. Several onlookers let out startled gasps. I stood paralyzed, pressed against Declan's chest, his heart thumping wildly against my back, in rhythm with mine.

"Jaysus," he finally muttered, his lips warm against my ear. He curled his fingers into my arms, not letting go. "Look left, not right. Or look *down*, to be sure." He gestured to the white writing on the road that read *Look Left* with an arrow reinforcing the direction.

I nodded faintly, swallowing the lump of panic in my throat. Taking a deep breath, I inhaled the woodsy, spicy scent of Declan's cologne, a more calming scent than the hotel spa. He'd smelled like freshly fallen rain the other day. I took another deep breath, my shoulders relaxing, my heart rate slowing. My life had flashed before my eyes, the highlight Malahide Castle. How sad was that? I wasn't ready to die. I had a ton more castles to visit.

"It's okay to cross now." Declan slowly released his grip on my arms.

My gaze darted left, right, left, right as I crossed the

street. I shoved the BEOs into my purse, not wanting to be distracted and collide with a bus or a tourist wandering aimlessly.

Declan snapped my picture with a street performer dressed in an oversized leprechaun costume.

I tossed a euro in the coin-filled, green velvet top hat on the ground. "You should have kept that leprechaun outfit. There's good money in it."

Dressing like a leprechaun appeared much more lucrative than dressing like an elf.

Declan dropped a coin in an empty coffee cup on the ground next to an artist painting a sprawling historical building with large stone pillars and statues in front. A crush of people carrying backpacks and totes were coming and going through the building's arched doorway, leading to a courtyard.

The guy gave Declan a surprised look. "Ah, thanks, mate."

As we walked away, I said, "I don't think he's looking for money."

"He needs it if he's attending Trinity College. I was once a starving artist."

"Did you go to school there?"

He shook his head. "Was never much into school."

"Do you sell your artwork? Have a website I can check out?"

"Don't draw anymore."

"Why not?"

He shrugged, raking a hand through his hair, gazing off into space.

Why didn't he want to discuss his art? If I had a natural talent for anything, I'd blab it to the world. I couldn't imagine giving up a passion like art.

We passed by a shop window displaying cozy wool sweaters and scarves. "Can we pop in here? I need a scarf." I'd left my ex while he was at work, and I'd packed my belongings in a mad frenzy, leaving behind my favorite scarf.

I turned back and entered the small shop with wool sweaters and ponchos stacked on tables and hanging on wall racks. I strolled down an aisle of scarves, Declan walking in front of me. Rather than checking out the scarves, I was checking out Declan's butt. This was the first time I'd seen him out of black slacks and in a pair of jeans that showed off his butt. He had a great butt. I was also wearing jeans. Had he been checking out *my* butt? He stopped to look at a sweater, and my gaze darted to a table of fashion scarves, a bright blue one catching my eye. I massaged the soft mohair fabric between my fingers.

"Try it on," Declan said.

It would make a serious dent in my souvenir budget. "I better stick with one of those fifteen-euro wool scarves."

He draped the lightweight mohair scarf around my neck. Staring deep into my eyes, he held the ends of the scarf, his hands brushing against my breasts, causing all my senses to go on red alert. "The color is brilliant on you. You should buy it."

"Kind of out of my budget," I muttered.

Yet I didn't take it off. I wasn't sure if it was because I didn't want Declan to remove his hands or because I desperately wanted the scarf.

He turned me toward a mirror, standing behind me, peering at us. "Buy it." He strolled off.

Declan was a total charmer and likely just trying to make me feel good, but I agreed the scarf was flattering, bringing out the blue in my eyes. I hadn't worn bright blue in a long time. My ex insisted it was a horrible color on me. More like it was my *best* color, but it'd been one more way for him to make me feel incompetent. That I didn't even have the ability to properly dress myself.

I marched over to the salesclerk and handed her cash, using most of Dad's fun money. My big splurge this trip.

A few blocks later, we encountered a two-story, glass-front store with an explosion of green souvenirs inside.

"Thought you might fancy another pair of leprechaun socks." Declan wore a teasing grin.

"Ha-ha."

We entered, and a guy handed me a green shopping basket. I thanked him, gazing around at sweatshirts, T-shirts, candy, jewelry, trinkets, and an entire wall dedicated to celebrating St. Paddy's Day with boas, garters, flashing ties, you name it.

The song "Galway Girl" played through the store.

"I love this song," I said. "I wonder if they have it on a CD."

"Since *P.S. I Love You* came out, it's on a lot of CDs."

"My friend Ashley and I watched that movie a dozen times. I've never read the book."

"Filming locations will be on our County Wicklow tour, no doubt."

"Do you think we'll get to go on the tour?"

"Of course—we'll have to escort it to make sure nobody is attacked by a mad sheep."

"Please tell me that's never happened."

He shrugged, a mischievous glint in his eyes.

Declan offered to run and buy the office supplies and snacks. I didn't argue, since it would take me hours to browse through the store. I debated a red-haired doll in a colorful step-dancing dress, but decided it wasn't practical.

Rachel had once brought me back a set of stack dolls from Russia. They still sat in a row on my dresser. For weeks, I'd drifted off to sleep staring at them, imagining the rural village where she'd bought them. A quaint shop on a narrow, cobblestoned street, where a little old lady sat on a stool hand painting the dolls, a craft that had been passed down through generations of her family. I now realized that Rachel had likely bought them at a hotel gift shop or the airport. She traveled the world, but how much of it did she actually see, working eighteen-hour days?

A rack displayed pins with Irish surnames, including Coffey. I decided on one for myself, Mom, and Rachel. I checked my phone, but still no e-mail from Mom. I tossed a Coffey coaster, keychain, and magnet in my basket. All the items bore the Coffey family crest—a green shield with three gold goblets, and a suit-of-armor helmet, bordered with a green-and-gold swirly design. How cool, and very medieval, that my family had a coat of arms. I suddenly felt a common bond to everyone with the Coffey surname, living and dead.

Finding a CD with "Galway Girl" was no problem,

except for the money. Outside of the few cheap surname trinkets, I needed to stick with necessities, like an umbrella with sheep on it and a green sweater on clearance for a steal. After carefully examining the sweater for flaws, I tossed it in my basket. I didn't own one green piece of clothing. Being Irish, I needed some green in my wardrobe.

I was debating between a pair of undies with sheep and one with lips that read *Póg Mo Thóin*, when Declan walked up and said, "Kiss my arse."

I gave him a baffled look, wondering where that comment had come from.

"That's what *Póg Mo Thóin* means."

"You know Gaelic?"

"We call it Irish, and I know a few choice words and phrases." He gave me a sly grin.

"How did you shop so fast?"

"It's been an hour." He held up several plastic bags bursting with office supplies and snacks. A card dropped from his hand.

I picked it up and read it. *As you slide down the banister of life, may the splinters never point in the wrong direction.*

I smiled, handing him the card. "Profound."

"It's my sister Zoe's birthday next week. It's an inside joke. She once slid down a wooden banister at our grandparents' and got a long sliver stuck in her arse. She almost had to go to the hospital to have it removed. She never lived that one down."

"How old will she be?"

"Twenty-five. Four years younger than me." He stared at the card, his smile fading. "If we hadn't been talking about her last night, I'd probably have forgotten her birthday. Guess I'm an even worse feckin' brother lately than I thought." He gestured to the *Póg Mo Thóin* undies. "Those are brilliant." He headed toward the checkout counter.

If Declan had guilt over being a bad brother and a bad grandson, having been gone when his grandma died, then why didn't he go home more often?

I grabbed the sheep undies. I walked away, then turned around and snagged the *Póg Mo Thóin* pair. Not because they were Declan's favorite, but I needed another pair. I left the store with under two hundred bucks left on my credit card, hoping that would last me until I got home.

"Fancy a pint?" Declan asked.

I could kill for a drink, but after my reaction to the way he'd stared into my eyes over the scarf, I was afraid to be alone with Declan, drinking on an empty stomach. Besides, I'd heard Gretchen ask him to meet for a drink. I was already on her shit list.

"That's okay. Go meet Gretchen. I'm going to take a walk."

"I'm not meeting Gretchen. She'd asked if I wanted to grab a pint later, but I didn't agree to."

"She already hates me. I don't need her thinking you ditched her to have a drink with me. I don't want to come between you two."

Declan's eyes widened. "You think I'm seeing Gretchen?" He looked seriously offended. "We had a one-night stand on a program last year, and it was a mistake. Too much Guinness."

Okay, so he'd merely *slept* with her once. At least he

thought it was a mistake. Yet I couldn't help but think Declan likely had women in every city from Dublin to Dubai. Wait, was Dubai a city or a small country? I made a mental note to Google Dubai. Regardless, he undoubtedly had a lot of one-night stands on programs, which showed a serious lack of respect for women.

A guy would never disrespect me again.

"It was kind of a rough day. I'd just like to take a walk by myself." I was directionally challenged, but I had a map, and someone could likely point me toward the hotel if needed.

"It's dark out and—"

"I'm allowed out after dark. I can take care of myself."

Declan snapped his mouth shut, holding his hands up in surrender.

Realizing my tone was sharper than I'd intended, I smiled. "I have a map. I'll be fine. The streets are busy. Why don't you meet up with your buddy from the pub the other night?" I was being nosey, fishing for the reason why he was avoiding that guy.

He shrugged off an uneasy look. "Maybe I will. Stick to the main streets, then. You've got my mobile number." He strolled down the sidewalk, and I averted my gaze from his butt.

At the end of the block, I peered down a side street, recognizing the Temple Bar area. I headed down the cobblestoned street lined with colorful restaurants and pubs, bustling with people. I stopped in front of Daly's pub, the location of our welcome dinner, a fiddle tune enticing me to go inside. I had never been in a bar by myself. When meeting friends, I always made sure I arrived a few minutes late so I wasn't stuck waiting by myself.

A group of laughing girls headed inside, and loneliness consumed me. It'd been over a year since I'd had a girls' night out. Ashley and I used to do Martini Mondays at a trendy downtown bar. We'd met weekly until I started dating my ex. Then it became once a month, once every other month...then never.

Grandma had sailed alone from Ireland to a strange land, her future unknown, and I couldn't even go into a pub by myself?

I marched inside before I could chicken out. People were clapping and singing along to a lively tune about saying good-bye to Muirsheen Durkin. I wasn't sure if that was a person or a place. Nobody noticed another tourist walking in, unlike a locals' bar, where I'd have stood out. I was relieved not to recognize the bartenders, who wouldn't know me as the Kildare Sausage. I slid up on a barstool, debating a Guinness or red wine. It had taken me a while to develop a taste for red wine. Maybe there was hope for Guinness.

I ordered a half-pint since I was down to twenty-three euros in cash.

Only a matter of minutes and a guy swooped in next to me. "Can I buy you a drink?"

Despite being broke, I wasn't in the mood to be hit on.

"*Je ne parle pas anglais.*" I smiled apologetically, pulling three college French semesters out of my butt. He gave me a confused and defeated look and headed on to his next victim.

I didn't know anybody there, and they didn't know me. I could be Monique Dubois, French socialite whose family owned a chain of poodle groomers. Or Sophie Bardot, notorious art forger whose forgeries hung in the unsuspecting, most stately homes in France. What better place to reinvent myself than a place where nobody knew me. I could be whoever I wanted to be.

I just had to figure out who that person was.

CHAPTER THIRTEEN

I only allowed myself one Guinness, not wanting to oversleep again and needing to find my way back to the hotel. Also, expensing alcohol wasn't allowed unless it was with a meal, and I didn't want to spend any of the remaining credit on my card for food. Thankfully, Declan had offered to expense our meals at the pub the other night.

Despite being a weeknight, the Temple Bar area was still packed with people coming and going and congregating outside pubs, smoking. I turned down a side street lit by streetlamps, with several couples on it. Partway down, the two couples ahead of me entered a building, and the couple across the street turned a corner. It suddenly didn't seem as well lit, with only me and one other person a half block behind me. I stopped, debating heading back to the busier street, and the person behind me stopped.

What the hell?

Too afraid to turn around, I continued on,

quickening my pace. Martha's warning about my ex, and the crazed look in his eyes, flashed through my mind. He could easily have discovered I'd gone to Dublin. He probably had connections with Homeland Security and could track my passport. Or he'd merely followed me to the airport. Heart thumping frantically against my chest, I held my purse in front of me, blindly rifling through it for my pepper spray. Luckily, Mom had insisted I pack it, thanks to Aunt Dottie's mugging.

At the corner, I made a sharp turn onto another dimly lit street, praying the person was a mugger and not my ex. How crazy was that? My breathing quickened, and I flattened myself against the side of the building, pepper spray raised, hoping he continued straight down the street. The steps drew nearer. He reached the corner and turned my way. I blasted him with pepper spray, then fled.

"Bloody hell! Feckin' A, Caity!"

Instead of my ex screaming out my name, it was Declan.

I stopped and spun around. "Omigod! What the hell are you doing?" I marched back to him and dropped my souvenir-filled bags at my feet.

He was coughing and pressing the heels of his hands into his eyes. "Good thing your"—he sucked in some serious air, then coughed—"aim is shite and"—another cough—"hit more of my hair than my face."

"I'm sorry, but I was scared shitless! I thought you were a mugger or my ex!" The uncontrollable shaking in my body had found its way to my voice, and my heart was ready to explode.

"Jaysus. I've pissed off some women, but never have they sprayed me with that shite." He attempted to clear the raspy sound from his throat. "What the hell did the wanker do to you?" He coughed. "And why would he be here?"

A warm tear slipped down my cheek, and I wiped away the moisture. I clamped my teeth down on my lower lip, stifling a sob.

Declan inhaled a ragged, calming breath, reining in his anger, obviously realizing how upset I was. He reached out to touch me, then snapped his hand back to catch a cough. "It's okay. I'm grand, see?" He struggled to keep his eyes open and choked back a cough.

I wanted Declan to console me. To wrap me in a warm embrace and assure me everything would be okay. Not just about my ex but my job, my finances, my relationship with Rachel, my life. However, the pepper spray fumes were making my eyes water even from a distance. I pulled a bottled water from my purse and handed it to him.

"Mightn't you have something stronger in there, like whiskey?"

I tried desperately to smile at his attempt to lighten the mood. He took a drink, then dropped his head back and poured water over his face, flushing out his eyes, blinking rapidly. He let out another cough.

"What if"—I choked down the lump in my throat—"you're blind?"

"I'm not blind. Can see you as plain as ever, I can."

"Why were you following me?"

He took the last sip of water and cleared his throat.

"Rachel went mad that you didn't return with me and told me to find you."

I was furious Rachel had sent Declan out searching for me because she didn't think I should be out alone after dark or was capable of finding my way back to the hotel.

Yet look at what had just happened!

"I was going pub to pub when you walked out of Daly's a block ahead of me." He coughed and swiped his hand under his nose. I didn't have any tissues to give him. "You've made it very clear you can take care of yourself, so I was going to follow you to make sure you got back okay. When you started walking faster, I was about to call out to you, until you sprayed me with that shite."

"I'm sorry."

"If your ex is stalking you, it's no wonder Rachel doesn't want you out walking alone."

My body went rigid. "Rachel doesn't know about my ex. And I'm sure he's not here. It's just my imagination running wild."

He looked skeptical.

"You have to promise not to say anything."

"How can I not say—"

"Promise," I demanded. "And don't ever mention this again. Pretend like it never happened."

His defeated sigh ended in a cough. "Fine, on one condition."

"What?" I said hesitantly, not in the mood for cutting deals.

"Let me take you back to the hotel."

I nodded faintly.

I was a hot mess, getting worse rather than better. I'd lost my ability to think rationally. My first instinct should have been that a mugger, not my ex, had been following me. My ex was not in Dublin. He wouldn't hurt me, if for no other reason than it would hurt his career and people's perception of him as a great guy. I had to stop letting him control my life when he wasn't even around. It felt like everyone was in control of my life except me!

I needed to control my life!

Declan couldn't see well enough to walk, and needed to shower off the pepper spray ASAP, so we took a taxi back to the hotel. I apologized again, which at least broke the awkward silence between us. He paid the taxi fare, making me feel even worse, but I didn't have money to argue.

When we walked into the hotel, I gasped at the sight of his puffy, bloodshot eyes and red inflamed skin.

"That bad, is it?" he asked.

I shook my head, looking away, praying we didn't see anyone we knew, especially Rachel.

We rode the elevator up together in silence. Declan said good night when he got off, but avoided my gaze.

Hopefully, I could trust Declan not to mention this evening to Rachel or me again. He was undoubtedly curious why I'd be blasting my ex with pepper spray. Although after all my screwups and going berserk over the walking tour, he probably thought I was a total

head case. I'd have crashed and burned day one
without his help. And that was the thanks he got for
once again coming to my rescue. Being blasted with a
debilitating spray.

I tossed my shopping bags on the bed. Still shaking
and on an adrenaline rush, I popped a sleeping pill and
made a cup of chamomile tea to relax. I placed the mug
on my Coffey coaster. I attached the Coffey pin to my
purse. I had no energy to write in my travel journal.
Besides, what was I going to write about? The first time
I'd zapped someone with pepper spray? The first time
I'd received a gift amenity, ate it, and it turned out not
to be mine? First time...

Stop reliving the day!

I opened my e-mail to find one from Mom. Aunt
Teri wasn't sure where she'd stashed the letters, but she
would try to find them. She didn't own a scanner, so
she'd have to photocopy them and stick them in the
mail. The only public photocopier in her small town
was at the library, open two days a week. For the love of
God. She only lived an hour from my parents. Couldn't
Mom drive over and pick up the letters if Teri found
them?

If my aunt *did* find them.

Mom didn't mention her grandparents' names. Did
that mean she didn't know their names or she'd
forgotten to answer my question? Or she didn't want to
learn about her mother's past? Yet she'd been going
through old photos and had attached one of Grandma
and Theresa, who the family had assumed was merely a
friend until finding the letters. It was the only photo
from Grandma's life in Ireland. Mom noted the date on

the back read 1935 and Grandma was nineteen. I used my phone's calculator to determine she'd been born in 1916. Grandma had also written that her dress was pink, her hat cream with a pink silk rose.

I opened the attachment to find a yellowed black-and-white photo of two slender, young women wearing bright smiles and mid-length dresses made with flowing fabric, probably chiffon. Long strands of beads hung around their necks, and cloche hats and light-colored, shoulder-length wavy hair framed their faces. Grandma had been quite the fashion diva and beautiful. I never knew Rachel and I had Grandma's heart-shaped face, which age and plumper features had softened.

A crowd of dressed-up people mingled behind them, in front of a church. Was it a family wedding? I scanned the crowd for possible relations who resembled Grandma or her sister. The faces weren't clear.

Grandma had looked so happy. What had happened? What had her family done that was so awful she'd claimed they were all dead? No matter how bad things got between Rachel and me, she'd never claim I was dead.

Would she?

The sleeping pill was kicking in, making the photo a blur. I double-checked that I'd locked the door. I grabbed the desk chair, preparing to wheel it over to the door, then stopped.

Not tonight.

My ex, *Andy*, was done controlling my life.

"Andy."

I spoke his name out loud with confident

determination, proving I could do it. I could say his name without throwing up. I refused to be one of those women who suffered from post-traumatic stress disorder for years, or even worse, forever! Martha had been encouraging me to join her women's therapy group. I hadn't gone, because the thought of spilling my guts to strangers gave me panic attacks. However, confiding in strangers now seemed easier than confiding in loved ones. After all, many of the women were in a similar situation as me and shared the same feelings. And maybe once I was comfortable openly discussing my emotions, I'd have an easier time telling people I knew.

I e-mailed Martha, inquiring when the next group met.

I let out a whoosh of air, dropping back in my chair, relieved yet nervous over having sent the e-mail. For now, I had to remind myself...

I was right.

I was strong.

I was worthy.

Andy could *Póg Mo Thóin*, as my undies said.

I put the *Kiss My Ass* undies on the bathroom counter for tomorrow. I should have bought a dozen pairs.

Who'd have thought undies could be so empowering?

CHAPTER
FOURTEEN

The next morning, an e-mail from Martha informed me that her therapy group was meeting the following week. She was proud of me for *taking this critical step toward recovery*. A nervous feeling fluttered in my chest, but I replied I'd be there, and hit send before I could back out.

I could do this.

I *had* to do this.

When I met with Martha, I could also discuss opportunities for counseling positions in Milwaukee and if I'd need a master's degree. I stood, then dropped back down onto the chair. Why put it off? I sent Martha another e-mail inquiring about a possible counseling career. I smiled with satisfaction, proud of my can-do attitude.

I left the maid a two-euro tip on the nightstand despite the travel letter stating Brecker was covering maid gratuities. I felt bad about rifling through her garbage in the hallway, even though I'd cleaned it up, and she'd left me more tea and lavender-scented toiletries for Martha's shelter.

I tied my new blue scarf around my neck. It didn't go with my black suit and white shirt, so I put in blue dangly earrings, attempting to tie the outfit together. Most importantly, I had on my *Póg Mo Thóin* undies, ready to conquer the world.

At least this job anyway.

I arrived at the office a half hour early and breathed a sigh of relief that Rachel was alone, typing away on her laptop, a mega-sized coffee next to her. I wanted to confront her about the whole Gretchen spa fiasco yesterday and clear the air. But I didn't think it bugged Rachel nearly as much as it did me. I'd stood up for myself, and that was what mattered.

I had to let it go.

"Morning," I said with a sunny smile.

Rachel glanced up, still typing. "Good morning." She peered back at her computer.

I booted up my laptop and showed her Grandma's photo. "Mom sent me this picture of Grandma and Theresa in Ireland, from 1935. Grandma was nineteen, so she was born in 1916."

Rachel stopped typing and studied the photo. "They looked a lot alike. Love the dresses and hats. Remember when Grandma used to let us dress up in her fancy hats she always wore to church?"

I nodded, smiling, even though I couldn't remember the hats. I'd only been seven, and my memory sucked. I was lucky I remembered the aprons. But I really wanted to remember the hats.

"Can you forward me the picture?"

"Sure." I gave her the pin I'd bought. "I popped into a gift shop last night that had a ton of Coffey stuff."

"How cool. Thanks."

Rachel held the pin between her fingers, massaging a thumb over it, as if she were trying to channel Grandma. Maybe she felt a connection to Grandma, having inherited her courage, determination, and sense of adventure. Whereas, I felt a connection, aspiring to be more like the woman I'd barely known.

"I still don't remember seeing her teacup since I moved." Worry creased Rachel's brow, and she typed a reminder in her phone to look for the teacup.

It gave me hope that the missing teacup bothered her.

Declan strolled in, his blue eyes no longer bloodshot, swollen, or showing any negative side effects of the pepper spray that would require an explanation. Thank God there was no permanent damage.

He eyed my new blue scarf with a smile. "Brilliant scarf."

"Thanks." Relief washed over me that he didn't appear to hold a grudge. "Come see the picture of our grandma."

He joined us at my computer. "Ah, lovely snap. I have one of my granny around that era."

"The same grandma whose banister Zoe slid down?" I asked.

Declan smiled reminiscently, nodding faintly.

"Who's Zoe?" Rachel asked.

"My sister."

"You have a sister?"

Declan nodded.

Rachel had mentioned having worked a half-dozen meetings with Declan, yet she hadn't known about Zoe?

"Do you know your granny's town yet?" he asked.

I let out an impatient groan. "No. Not yet."

Declan went to schmooze VIPs at breakfast. Minutes later, Kathleen Reynolds entered the office and requested walking directions to their restaurant that evening. Rachel closed Grandma's photo.

"Omigosh, Caity, what a lovely scarf. Did you buy it here? It'd go perfectly with the dress I'm wearing to dinner tonight."

I nodded. "At a wool shop ten minutes away. Declan might recall the name."

"Would you like her to pick you up one?" Rachel asked.

"Or I could take you to the shop," I said.

My heart raced while I stood paralyzed with fear.

Had I just offered to take the CEO's wife shopping?

From the panicked look in Rachel's eyes, I had. After finding one lost cell phone, I suddenly thought I was qualified to handle VIP needs? If I was going to prove to Rachel that I could do this job, I couldn't avoid the attendees, not even the VIPs.

Kathleen smiled brightly. "That'd be great. You're the same size as my daughter, Alyssa. I'd love to have your help picking out some sweaters for her. If you have the time, of course."

"Absolutely," I said. I could see the hesitation on Rachel's face, afraid to send me off with the CEO's wife.

Not as afraid as I was to *go* off with the CEO's wife. One wrong turn and we might end up in a sketchy area. Getting mugged. Getting—

"Could you meet me in the lobby at nine?" Kathleen asked.

I plastered on a perky smile. "Sure, see you then."

She left, and I stifled a distressed squeak.

Rachel's gaze darted to me. "What were you thinking, offering to take her shopping?"

I shrugged—no clue what I'd been thinking! "I thought it would be a nice thing to do. That she'd appreciate the special attention."

"I'm sure she does, but it's not like you're in Milwaukee, a city you actually know." She shook her head in disbelief, blowing out a frustrated sigh, then regained her professional composure. "Doesn't matter now. We'll figure it out. Do you remember how to get to the store?"

"Not exactly. But Declan does."

Rachel phoned Declan and asked him to report to the office pronto. He arrived within minutes, and she explained the situation. We determined that using my phone's map app would be insanely expensive. So Declan highlighted the route to the shop on a city map.

"Are you sure you're clear on how to get there?" Rachel asked.

"Yes," I said with way more confidence than I felt.

"Reading a map might be confusing when you don't know Dublin." Rachel looked at Declan. "Maybe you should write out the directions. Like, take a left onto this street, then go two blocks to this street, et cetera."

How about Declan just went with and held my hand crossing the street? Or better yet, he could put me on one of those leashes parents led their kids around on at the zoo or amusement park, to make sure I didn't get lost.

Rachel's phone rang on her desk, and she reluctantly stepped away to answer it.

"Told you that scarf looks brilliant on you. Glad you bought it, aren't you now?"

No. Because *now* I had to take the CEO's wife shopping. I wanted to ask Declan to take her. He knew the store's location. But after yesterday's blowup over the walking tour, demanding he back off, and then pepper spraying him, I couldn't play the damsel in distress.

I had to prove I could do this myself.

Hopefully, I could.

Declan gave me a reassuring smile. "Talk to her like a regular person, not like she's the bloody Queen of England. Just be yourself. You'll be grand."

Omigod, I was going to have to *talk* to her.

I'd been so worried about walking her to the store, I hadn't even thought about what I'd say to her. What if I couldn't think of anything to discuss and we wandered around Dublin in awkward silence? Even worse, what if I said something stupid or unprofessional?

Declan's gaze narrowed with concern. "Would you like me to take her?"

My panic was obviously transparent. But did he think I was afraid to be on the streets with the CEO's wife or my ex on the loose? Or that I wasn't capable of doing it?

Stop looking freaked out!

"Thanks, but she wants me to try on sweaters for her daughter, and you probably aren't the same size. I'll try hard not to wander into a sketchy area." I laughed off the possibility with more of a nervous giggle than an amused one.

"You'd have to wander pretty far from here to hit a dodgy area."

That eased a little bit of the tension in my neck.

Declan slid a discreet glance toward Rachel, still on the phone, then leaned in and whispered, "Can't go as bad as the time I nearly killed a CEO."

My gaze narrowed. "Literally? On purpose?"

A mysterious glint sparkled in his blue eyes, and he walked out.

I couldn't believe he'd left me hanging like that! But it did make me feel better. Unless I tripped and accidentally pushed Kathleen in front of a double-decker bus, I didn't foresee me causing her death. Although I had to remember to look in the opposite direction for oncoming traffic, or I might *walk* her out in front of a bus.

Rachel set down her phone and waved me over, undoubtedly wanting to drill me on the directions to the shop.

"Watch out for Declan," she said.

My gaze narrowed in confusion. "What are you talking about?"

"The whole 'that scarf looks brilliant on you.' Not that it doesn't. He's a nice guy but a total player. I've heard stories."

I rolled my eyes. "From Gretchen, I'm sure."

"And several others."

Several others? That was kind of what I had figured.

"Don't worry. There's nothing going on between us."

Rachel's instincts had been dead-on about my ex, or rather Andy. Was she also right about Declan? I couldn't imagine ever again trusting a guy or my judgment of one. Didn't matter. There seriously was nothing going on. Hopefully, Declan had better morals when it came to keeping secrets than he did with keeping his pants on.

CHAPTER
FIFTEEN

Luckily, Kathleen talked nonstop our entire walk to the shop, so I didn't have to make idle chitchat. I was half listening, needing to stay focused on our route. The nervous flutter in my chest finally subsided when I spotted the familiar green storefront with lovely wool sweaters in the window. I'd escorted Kathleen to the shop without making one wrong turn or stepping into traffic. Phew.

We entered the shop, and I headed straight for the stack of scarves. No blue scarf. I rifled through the scarves, making sure one wasn't hidden. Would Rachel expect me to give Kathleen mine? I didn't want to give up my scarf. I wasn't sure how far Rachel would go for a VIP.

A young salesclerk eyed the scarf disaster but gave me a cheery smile, assuring me she had more blue scarves in back. She went in search of them. Within minutes, she returned with two blue scarves. Kathleen took one for herself and one for her daughter, Alyssa.

She also picked out a brown-and-blue plaid scarf that went nicely with her stylish outfit—dark jeans, a brown tweed blazer, navy shirt, and brown boots. I felt like a dork next to her in my black-and-white uniform with my blue scarf that didn't match. She had me try on a maroon wool poncho for Alyssa. I snuggled into the cozy garment, not wanting to take it off. The color looked *brilliant* with my auburn hair, as Declan would say. Unable to fork over a hundred and fifty euros for a poncho, I reluctantly slipped it off and handed it to Kathleen.

She insisted on buying me something for my troubles. I assured her that wasn't necessary. And I didn't want to lose my job by accepting gifts if it was frowned upon. She pushed the matter until I finally agreed to an inexpensive purple wool scarf. Surely Rachel would be okay with that.

If she found out.

We left and a block later encountered an upscale shop where Kathleen dropped more on a set of Waterford Crystal wineglasses than I'd spent on all my souvenirs.

Next we passed by a corner restaurant with a red exterior and red and purple potted petunias hanging along the front.

"Oh, how cute is this? Let's do lunch." Kathleen zipped inside before I could respond.

A gentleman in a black suit, with a French accent rather than an Irish one, led us through the restaurant done in red furnishings, white linens, and red walls filled with autographed celebrity photos—some of whom I recognized. He seated us at a window table with a pre-theater menu. We were apparently in the theater district, the reason for the celebrity photos.

I excused myself and made a beeline for the bathroom to call Rachel.

"She wants to do lunch. Is that okay?"

"That's fine."

"It looks like a crazy-expensive place."

"Put it on your credit card and expense it."

My credit card? My heart raced.

"If that's not okay, I can pop over and give them my card."

"No, that's fine."

This lunch would likely deplete the available credit on my card. No way could I tell Rachel that. I could call Declan and ask him to come to my rescue. However, I was sending him some serious mixed signals.

What the hell was I going to do?

This was lunch, not dinner. Maybe it wouldn't be too expensive.

I returned to the table to find Kathleen sipping a white wine, with a glass of wine sitting at my place. It wasn't even noon. I couldn't drink on the job, could I? And I preferred red.

"I hope you like the wine," Kathleen said. "If not, get something else, and I'll drink it."

I took a sip of the sweet wine, freaking out over how expensive it tasted. I'd have to blame my credit card company for denying my charge, despite having advised them of my travels abroad. I scanned the menu for the cheapest item, a bowl of Irish seafood chowder.

"Thanks so much for shopping with me. I miss girls' days out with Alyssa." Kathleen took a drink of wine, then stared longingly at the glass. "I hardly see her since she went off to college last year. And Tom doesn't get it. He says I need to give her space. Can you believe that?"

"That's a man for you."

That was the CEO. What if she told her husband, *I had lunch with Caity, and she agrees that you're an insensitive jerk*? I had to watch what I said. I also didn't want Tom to think I'd been out boozing it up with her.

"Exactly." She polished off her wine and gestured to the waiter for another. "Sometimes he's so unsympathetic, I could leave him." She glanced down at the three-carat rock on her finger. "You know what I mean?"

Whoa. The conversation had officially veered outside my comfort zone. I was a scorned woman and would like nothing more than a lively bout of men bashing, except when the CEO and my job were involved.

"Where's Alyssa going to school?" I asked, attempting to get the conversation back on track.

"Madison. Too far. I feel like we're growing apart." She reminisced about attending the *Nutcracker* every Christmas since Alyssa was little. The two of them vacationing in Italy. And their weekend shopping trips to Chicago. The waiter brought her more wine, and she took a gulp. A tear slipped down her cheek.

I shifted in my chair, taking a sip of wine. I never knew how to react when people cried. Did Kathleen want me to console her with a hug or ignore her tears? Was it appropriate to hug a client? Ugh. I never doubted Mom's love for us, but she wasn't a hugger, and growing up we'd received few words of sympathy. If we scraped a knee or had a fight with a friend, she was more the *suck it up* type mom. Oddly enough, she was overbearing, yet we weren't brought up to openly discuss our feelings. I'd told her the bare minimum about Andy because her friend had landed me the job and I also had to warn her in case he showed up on their doorstep.

Kathleen bent over and rifled through her purse on the floor, searching for a tissue. I swooped in and poured some of her wine in my water glass, which was now full. I glanced around to see if anyone was watching, unable to believe I'd just done that. I eyed the centerpiece, daffodils in a crystal vase, with room for wine. I slipped off my suit jacket, starting to sweat.

She finally found a tissue and blew her nose.

"I rarely came home when I first went to college, wanting to be independent. And now I'm living back home."

This news perked Kathleen up, while making me want to slam my glass of wine. "So your mom and you are close again?"

I nodded. Closer than we'd been since I'd started dating Andy anyway.

"I only want what's best for Alyssa."

Same as Mom, but that was difficult to remember when she was calling and e-mailing me a dozen times a day and playing career counselor. Mom had likely been this upset over me moving in with Andy and rarely seeing her. Had she had a similar meltdown at Aunt Teri's kitchen table, wondering where she'd gone wrong that both her daughters had abandoned her? My chest tightened at the thought of causing Mom so much pain. If she'd explained how she'd felt, maybe I'd have snapped out of my brainwashed state of mind.

"Tell Alyssa how you feel," I said. "That you want to give her freedom—you just don't want to grow apart. That your relationship is important to you."

Not real profound advice. However, a faint smile curled Kathleen's lips, and she was no longer crying. "You're right. We should talk about it."

Maybe Mom and I needed a girls' day out to do lunch and have fun without discussing psycho Andy or my lack of employment and future prospects.

Lunch arrived along with Kathleen's third glass of wine. She had grilled salmon on a bed of rice. My Irish seafood chowder contained several types of fish, scallops, shrimp, bacon, and potatoes. It was delish, though a small serving. I used the brown bread to wipe every creamy drop from the bowl.

Our conversation focused on Alyssa's degree and her high aspirations for a career after college. Sounded like me when I'd first entered college, before reality had set in. Kathleen insisted we share an order of macaroons, her favorite dessert, and she had a Baileys coffee.

I couldn't win. Except she insisted on paying the bill. I didn't argue, since it would max out my credit card. Hopefully, Rachel would approve.

On the way back to the hotel, Kathleen failed to realize we'd passed by the same fiddle player in a green kilt three times, even though she'd tossed a euro in his fiddle case each encounter and had a picture taken with him once. I wanted her to walk off as much alcohol as possible. Rather than being stumbling drunk and slurring her words, she was giddy, chatting incessantly about nothing. Better than talking smack about her husband.

By the time we reached the hotel, she seemed fairly sober, until she couldn't decide which elevator bank went to her room, so I escorted her. When we arrived at her room, she slipped the key in the door, but it wouldn't open.

"These keys are such a pain in the ass. They never work." She started pounding on the door. "Tom."

Omigod, Tom was there? My heart raced. Why wasn't he over at Flanagan's brewery? Although she likely had no clue as to the time and that Tom wasn't back yet.

"I'll go get a new key," I said.

The door next to us opened, and Tom poked out his head, looking annoyed, his cell phone to his ear. Nothing said *I'm drunk* like trying to break into the wrong room. Kathleen gave me a hug, thanked me for a great girls' day out, then raised her nose in the air, snubbing her husband as she brushed past him with her hands full of bags. I could just hear her repeating our conversation about him being an insensitive jerk. I wanted to offer to take a breathalyzer test so at least he knew *I* wasn't drunk! Tom eyed her with disapproval, then flashed me a look I couldn't decipher, before shutting the door. Embarrassment? Disappointment? Anger? What did that look mean?

I ran to my room, brushed my teeth, and popped a mint, hoping Rachel wouldn't smell wine on my breath.

I entered the office, and Rachel sprang from her chair, an apprehensive look on her face. "How'd it go?"

"Great." I could feel sweat beading above my upper lip.

Her gaze narrowed. "Really? You need to tell me if it didn't. She doesn't seem as difficult as the last CEO's wife, Natalie, who we called *Bat*alie."

I had to tell Rachel the truth. It wasn't like I'd had any control over Kathleen drinking. I'd handled the situation as well as possible. But would Rachel agree?

"She's really nice. She had a few glasses of wine and insisted on paying the bill. Wouldn't take no for an answer. She—"

"I'm so glad everything went well. Great job."

Rachel didn't seem concerned about Kathleen having paid the bill or her drinking, too focused on the fact we'd made it back alive. Luckily, she didn't ask if *I'd* drank. She let out a relieved sigh, as if she'd been holding her breath since I'd left.

She seemed so pleased I decided not to tell her about Tom. Besides, if Tom was pissed, I'd be fired. And if I told Rachel, she'd wig out and fire me, afraid that Tom was upset. I was fairly sure that Tom wouldn't mention the situation to anyone and wouldn't want me mentioning it. And he wouldn't bring up my garbage meltdown either. So much for me promising Rachel I wouldn't keep anything from her.

The secrets just kept piling up.

Declan and Gretchen walked in.

"Didn't end up in a dodgy end of town then, did ya?" Declan asked.

Rachel smiled. "She did a fabulous job."

Maybe I'd be promoted from sausage and bathroom attendant to VIP duty. God, I hoped not.

But if I was, it would no longer send me into a complete and utter panic.

Chapter Sixteen

The only hint Rachel offered about our dinner restaurant was that it was located within walking distance of the hotel. My grumbling stomach hoped it was merely across the street. The Irish seafood chowder and two macaroons earlier had been more like an appetizer than a meal. We walked along the Liffey, lit by streetlamps and several boats cruising slowly up the river. Thanks to a faint drizzle, I was able to use my new umbrella with one black sheep among dozens of white ones. I hadn't realized how symbolic a black sheep umbrella was for me when I'd bought it.

We were out of uniform, in jeans. Rachel had on black boots and a red sweater. Gretchen wore a slutty low-cut, tight-fitting purple sweater. I had on a jean jacket, a cream lace blouse, my new blue scarf, and brown boots. Declan had on a blue Leinster-logoed sweatshirt, and his jeans once again showed off his butt.

"Is that your favorite soccer team?" I asked him.

He smiled. "It's rugby."

"Is there a big difference?"

His smiled widened. "Yeah. It's more like American football without all the padding."

"Do you play?"

He shook his head. "I was in hurling growing up. That's with a stick."

"Like hockey?"

"It's played on grass, not ice. I'll give you a lesson in Irish sports sometime."

"And I'll give you a lesson in American football. My dad has season Packers tickets. I freeze my ass off at games twice a year." Although I hadn't the past two seasons because Andy despised football and its *beer-belching fans*, as he called them. I'd let that keep me from hanging out with Dad.

Not this season.

Declan looked impressed that I followed sports.

"Are we going to The Brazen Head?" Gretchen was undoubtedly trying to get off the subject of sports. If she had anything to contribute to the topic, she'd be dominating the conversation.

Rachel shrugged, wearing a teasing smile. "Maybe."

"The Brazen Head is Ireland's oldest pub," Declan told me.

"Remember the night you almost closed the place and we were dancing by the stage?" Gretchen asked Rachel.

My shock was obviously transparent. Rachel quickly added, "Attendees were gone, and we were staying an extra day."

I still couldn't picture it.

"The lead singer was totally into you," Gretchen said.

"No, he wasn't." Rachel shook her head.

"You could have had an Irish boyfriend if you'd wanted one."

"I don't have time for an *American* boyfriend, let alone hauling my ass across the ocean for one."

Rachel hadn't had a steady boyfriend in four years. After dating for ten months, Simon had dumped her when she'd called him bitching about her job while he'd been sitting in a restaurant, waiting for her to celebrate his birthday, which she'd forgotten.

"He wouldn't have to be a *boyfriend*," Gretchen teased.

I did a mental eye roll. Of all people to have the *love 'em and leave 'em* attitude, when she wouldn't *leave* Declan alone after a one-night stand. I glanced discreetly over at Declan, wondering if he was thinking the same thing. He was focused on a boat cruising slowly up the Liffey, likely tuning out Gretchen.

We walked across a bridge, then headed down a side street away from the river. A few blocks later we came across a green pub with gold lettering reading *Coffey's*.

"This is it," Rachel said.

Gretchen's forehead wrinkled. "I've never heard of this place."

"Neither had I. Found it through the hotel's concierge." Rachel peered over at me. "Thought we might be related to the owner."

I smiled. "How cool would that be?"

I couldn't believe Rachel had taken the initiative to find a pub with our Coffey surname. A lump of emotion lodged in my throat over Rachel treating me like a close sister rather than an incompetent employee.

"Do you have any Irish in your family?" I asked Gretchen.

"I'm not sure," she said.

She knew damn well she didn't have any Irish ancestry. If she did, she'd be bragging about it, giving her something in common with Declan.

It gave *me* something in common with Declan.

Declan held the door open, and lively chatter poured out of the pub rather than traditional Irish music. Not a touristy area, locals filled the wooden bar and booths, meeting friends for a pint after work. The walls displayed soccer, rugby, and hurling team photos, pennants, and jerseys. We snagged three stools at the end of the long bar. Declan stood, and Rachel sat on the middle stool, strategically separating Gretchen and me, undoubtedly realizing the friction between us.

I was unable to recall the last time Rachel and I'd gone drinking together. Probably Aunt Irene's Thanksgiving dinner. Aunt Irene was a horrible cook. One year she hadn't thawed the turkey enough, and it took an extra three hours to cook. An extra three hours we'd had to tolerate our obnoxious uncle Benny's crude pilgrim jokes and him cussing out the football refs on TV. Rachel and I'd offered to make a beer run to the grocery store up the street, and on our way home we stopped at a bar for hot toddies and a reprieve from Uncle Benny. My aunt hadn't hosted Thanksgiving dinner in three years.

Rachel's phone dinged, signaling a text. She read it, a smile spreading across her face. She glanced over at me. "Grandma's teacup is at the back of my kitchen cupboard. I asked my neighbor with a key to go look for it."

A warm feeling washed over me. Rachel's search for the teacup gave me even more hope of us reconnecting.

The bartender was fortyish, dark hair, blue eyes, and a firm jaw with a five o'clock shadow. He was fit, like he worked out lifting kegs of Guinness, rather than pints.

"Do you sell anything with Coffey on it, mate?" Declan asked. "Like your shirt." He gestured to the guy's green *Coffey's Dublin* T-shirt

"My grandma was a Coffey." I proudly pointed out the Coffey pin on my purse.

"Ah, grand," the guy said, despite the fact I was probably the dozenth person in there that day claiming Coffey ancestry. "We had T-shirts but been out for a spell now."

"How much for your shirt?" Rachel asked.

"Not for sale, luv. Only one more at home."

"I'll give you thirty euros."

He let out a hearty laugh. "Now what will you be having, besides my shirt?"

"Forty euros?" Rachel flashed him a smile.

He laughed, shaking his head.

Rachel flirted like I'd never seen her flirt. He walked to the back and returned a few minutes later wearing an Ireland sports jersey and tossed his Coffey T-shirt on the bar. "There, don't ever say an Irishman wouldn't be giving you the shirt off his back."

She slid forty euros across the bar, and he pushed it back with a wink. "I won't be taking advantage of a lovely lass."

"Thanks." Rachel smiled, blushing. Omigod, Rachel was blushing? She handed me the shirt, which held the scent of musk cologne rather than beer. "Welcome to Ireland."

I stared in awe at the shirt, as if she'd given me a priceless Irish family heirloom passed down through generations of Grandma's family. "Thanks."

The bartender shook Rachel's hand. "Gerry Coffey from County Cork. So whereabouts did your Coffeys hail from?"

Rachel looked to me for an answer.

"Mom never got back to me. County Westmeath, but I don't know the town." I texted Mom to see if she had any further info.

"What will you be having?" Gerry asked me.

"Food. And a Brecker Dark." I wasn't sure if we were required to drink Brecker when we were off duty. Were we ever really off duty?

Gerry's gaze narrowed. "Never heard of it."

"Really? It's the best. Way better than Guinness."

A young guy next to me said, "Better than Guinness, you say?"

"It's brilliant," I said.

"You best be looking into that, Gerry," the guy said.

"We should go pub-hopping and order Brecker Dark," I told Rachel. "If they don't have it, we can rave about it and convince the bartender to carry it."

Rachel's face lit up. "Great marketing idea." She slipped a business card from her purse and slid it across the bar to Gerry. "Brecker now owns Flanagan's. Check it out."

He snatched up the card, a glint in his eyes. "I will."

I wasn't sure if they were referring to checking out the beer or each other.

We ordered food and Flanagan's hard cider, except Declan had a whiskey. I took a drink of cider, and a sweet apple flavor filled my mouth, much lighter than Guinness. Not even a week in Ireland and I was becoming a beer connoisseur.

My phone dinged, signaling the arrival of a text. Mom.

"She says her grandparents were Patrick and Mary Coffey. Teri hasn't located the letters or naturalization papers yet, so she doesn't know Grandma's town."

What the hell was taking her so long?

"Now that you have their names, we can check the 1911 census," Declan said. "Do you think her parents were married by then?"

I shrugged. No clue.

Rachel's cell rang out on the bar next to her pint. My body went rigid, not wanting our fun to end. And not wanting the caller to be Tom Reynolds firing me for getting his wife drunk. She stepped outside to take the call. She returned a few minutes later with little stress lines creasing her forehead. She polished off her beer, rather than beating the pavement back to the hotel in crisis mode or firing me per Tom's request. I relaxed on my stool.

Gerry promptly brought her another cider.

Rachel raised her glass. "Here's to Caity, for escorting Kathleen Reynolds around Dublin like a true local."

"Here, here." Declan raised his glass.

"Absolutely." Gretchen smiled faintly.

I enjoyed the positive recognition, since it might be short lived. Recalling Declan and Gretchen's toast the other night, I said, *"Sláinte!"*

"You helped her feel better about her daughter going off to college," Declan said. I'd mentioned our conversation briefly to him earlier, leaving out the drinking part. "See, you can help women in this job. No need to be a counselor."

He was giving me more credit than I deserved. My counseling had merely consisted of advising Kathleen to talk to her daughter, because I wished Mom had talked to me. Not real profound.

Rachel gave me a curious look, unaware of my aspiration to be a counselor, since I hadn't even considered the career until yesterday. Still, it sometimes seemed like Declan knew me better than she did, same as Gretchen knew Rachel better than I did.

Hopefully, that would change.

I had the feeling Rachel and I might actually bond, thanks to our Irish grandma we'd barely known.

CHAPTER
SEVENTEEN

When we arrived back at the hotel, Rachel and Gretchen headed toward their guest-room elevator on the opposite side of the lobby as Declan's and mine.

"It's early," Declan said. "How about researching your granny?"

"Sure." After hanging out at Coffey's pub, I was psyched to learn more about Grandma's past.

"My room or yours?"

I sobered instantly, despite two pints of hard cider. Of course we'd have to go to one of our rooms to use a computer.

He gave me a curious smile. "Afraid you left your knickers lying around?"

"Yeah, I was trying to remember what shape my room is in."

"Right, then. My room is grand. We'll go there."

Declan acted like it was no big deal, like he had no ulterior motive for inviting me to his room. Of course he didn't. If for no other reason, I was Rachel's sister.

He wouldn't jeopardize his job by having a fling with me and possibly ticking me off.

Possibly being blasted with pepper spray again.

We entered his room, much tidier than mine, and tidier than I expected, considering he only ironed the front of his shirts. The duvet was folded neatly on a chair, with a note telling housekeeping to leave it off the bed.

"Too warm with the comforter on?" I asked.

"Too dodgy. Never know when it last saw the wash. I'm not a germophobe, but travel too much to get sick. I sanitize the phones and telly remote."

I hadn't disinfected a thing in my room. What rare, incurable disease was I going to contract?

"And best to sanitize the drinking glasses with a bit of whiskey before using them," he said with a sly grin.

"They don't change the glasses?"

"See any glasses on the housekeeping carts, do ya?"

During my one encounter with a housekeeping cart, I'd been too frazzled to pay attention to anything besides my garbage. I thought about the hotel robe I'd worn nightly.

"Do you think they wash the robes after someone checks out?"

He shrugged, looking skeptical.

I should have been more cautious. I never even used the plastic cover on a public toilet seat, for fear it was the same piece of plastic going around and around.

Declan sat at the desk and booted up his laptop. He searched Ireland's 1911 census for Patrick and Mary Coffey while I waited anxiously behind him.

"Patrick and Mary were very common names," he

said. "Coffey wasn't, yet there were several couples with those names in Westmeath." He scanned the records. "Here's one with a daughter Theresa born 1911."

A sense of excitement zipped through me. "Theresa was older than my grandma, so that could be her sister. And there's an Ellen, two years old. My mom's middle name is Ellen. Probably named after my grandma's sister. I'm sure she never knew that. My grandma couldn't have hated her sisters to have named her kids after them."

"So it's likely her family. Their eldest child, Michael, was four years old. They lived in Killybog, County Westmeath. It's on the border of Meath and Westmeath, under a half hour from where I grew up. Our rellies were practically neighbors. Might still be since many people farm their ancestors' land."

"Maybe our families knew each other. Have you ever been to Killybog?"

"Loads of times. My mate Peter is a publican there. It's been a few years since I've seen him. We were good mates in school."

"What's a publican?"

"Means he owns a pub."

"How couldn't my grandma have been happy living in a town named Killybog? Is it as cute and quaint as it sounds?"

Declan nodded. "I'll show you." He pulled up Google Maps and clicked on a small icon of a man in the lower corner and dragged it over to Killybog on the map. Suddenly, we were cruising down the streets of Grandma's hometown.

"Omigod." My eyes widened in awe. "I never knew

you could do that." My gaze swept down a street lined with colorful storefronts, including a blue building with a red door and gold lettering reading *Molloy's*.

"Molloy's is Peter's place."

I studied an old stone church located at the end of the street. "Is that the church from my grandma's photo? Can you zoom in?" I connected to the hotel's Wi-Fi on my phone and downloaded the pic Mom had sent me. It was indeed the same arched doorway, stained-glass windows, and steeple reaching up into the sky.

"I attended a funeral there several years ago."

I gasped, my gaze darting to Declan. "What did it look like inside?"

His gaze narrowed in contemplation. "Ah...it had pews, an altar... It looked like a church."

I let out a disappointed sigh, as if Declan's memories of the place would provide insight into Grandma. Though it was cool that he'd been in the same church Grandma once had.

"That's the only street in town," he said.

"I can look at it more later."

I had a feeling I wouldn't be getting any sleep tonight.

Declan returned to the census and pulled up the original document. I leaned in, peering over his shoulder, squinting to read the faint handwriting that noted the birth county for each family member, whether they could read or write, their occupations, et cetera. Declan turned his head toward me, our noses just inches apart. We stared into each other's eyes, his breath warm against my face, but not warm enough to be causing the heat rushing through me. He seriously had the thickest lashes ever. He glanced down at my lips, and I instinctively licked them. His gaze still glued to my mouth, he leaned in closer, his lips just shy of touching mine. My heart raced. My mouth went dry with anticipation.

Declan was going to kiss me.

I closed my eyes, preparing for the kiss. He snapped back, and my eyes shot open. His panicked gaze darted to the computer.

I slowly straightened, trying to focus on the census rather than the woodsy, spicy scent of Declan's cologne. And the fact that he'd almost kissed me.

Declan finally broke the awkward silence. "It says your granny's mom, Mary, was from County Wicklow. Too bad it doesn't have the town. We might drive through it on our tour tomorrow and not even know."

Visiting my great-grandma's homeland was even more exciting than seeing the filming locations for *P.S. I Love You.*

Heart still racing from our near kiss, I fought to keep the nervous flutter in my chest from floating up my throat to my voice. "She probably came from a large family if there were already three kids, and my grandma wasn't born for another five years. Why hadn't she wanted to come back to visit them? Why'd she claim they were all dead?"

Declan continued staring at the computer, avoiding my gaze. "You might be better off not knowing. When I helped my granny with her ancestry research, I discovered her dad hadn't died when she was two, like her mum claimed. He ran off with the pastor's wife."

"Omigod, your poor grandma. How did she handle the news?"

"I never told her. She was eighty-two. I figured, why upset her at that point in life. Not only would she hate a dad she never knew but be upset her mum never told her the truth. Let her think he died."

I nodded. "You're probably right. But unless it's really bad, I'm telling my mom. Hopefully, it helps her better understand why her mom was so distant. Why she left Ireland and what she was trying to escape from. I came to Ireland to escape my life, but not forever."

Declan finally met my gaze, quirking a curious brow. *Exactly why did I want to escape my life? My ex?*

"I should go," I said before he could question me or mention last night.

"Right, then. We can always research civil registration records later to track the family's marriages and deaths. But that's a bit time consuming and costly. When I researched my granny's rellies, I about went mad with paper trails. Probably easier for me to contact my mate Peter. It's a rural area. People know each other for kilometers. Might even be some Coffeys sitting in his pub. I'll e-mail him straight away."

"Thanks, I appreciate it." Our gazes locked, and heat rushed to my cheeks once again. "See you tomorrow." I bolted toward the door.

"Wait." Declan stood and walked toward me.

Heart racing, I stared at the door, debating fleeing or turning to face him and whatever this attraction was between us. Hadn't I just told myself I wasn't going to be a one-night stand, allowing a guy to take advantage of me? I had to be strong. I slowly turned to him, prepared to explain why I couldn't stay.

"I have something for you." He stepped into the bathroom and returned, handing me the hotel's lavender toiletries. "Here. For your friend's shelter."

I had never been more attracted to a man in my life.

"Thanks," I muttered, then turned and fled.

I flew down the hallway, squeezing the toiletry bottles in my trembling hands. If Declan was as big of a player as Rachel claimed, why hadn't he kissed me? What was wrong with me? Besides that I was a neurotic mess. Not to mention I'd blasted him with pepper spray. Was he now a bit gun-shy perhaps?

Not as gun-shy as I was.

❧ ❧

I stashed the soft velvet robe back in my closet, gagging at the thought of it not having been washed when the previous guest had slipped it on after showering. My adrenaline rush over visiting Coffey's pub, discovering Grandma's hometown, and my near kiss with Declan was winning the battle against exhaustion and two pints of cider. I debated washing out my new Coffey's T-shirt in the sink so I could wear it. However, I was only out of uniform a few hours a day.

And I was leaving Ireland in three days.

Melancholy zapped my adrenaline rush, and I sank onto the chair in front of my laptop. Before I left, I wanted to rent a car and drive to Killybog, except I had no money for a rental and I'd have to be suicidal to attempt driving on the opposite side of the road when I couldn't even *walk* safely across a road here. Besides, what would I do when I got to Killybog? Grandma had left there almost eighty years ago. What were the chances she still had relatives in the area?

I e-mailed the 1911 census link to Mom and Rachel, not mentioning I'd been alone in Declan's room researching our family tree. Rachel would go berserk after she'd warned me about him. I pointed out that Grandma had a sister Ellen, Mom's middle name. I crossed my fingers that Mom wouldn't find it too upsetting that she'd been named after an aunt she never knew existed.

Rachel responded to my e-mail almost immediately, thanking me, promising we'd chat more about it later. No surprise she was still online, working, no doubt.

An e-mail from Martha popped into my inbox, answering my questions on becoming a counselor. She advised me that she had an undergraduate degree. A master's wasn't required unless I wanted a job with a clinic or hospital as a mental health counselor, which entailed developing client treatment plans and billing insurance companies, for which I also needed to be licensed by the state. Jobs weren't plentiful, so I had to be willing to possibly relocate to Madison or Chicago. The prospect of starting fresh in another city was an enticing idea, except for the paying-rent part, especially since she also mentioned it wasn't the best-paying profession. However, any profession was better paying than none, and being able to help women would be fulfilling and give me a sense of purpose. She suggested we further discuss my counseling aspirations when we met next week at her therapy group and that she'd be happy to mentor me.

I replied, thanking her for the info and offering to be my mentor. I was totally psyched about my new career goal.

I returned to my ancestry research. I Googled Coffey, County Westmeath—discovering a slew of Westmeath genealogy forums. I excitedly clicked on one. Hundreds of messages had been posted over a ten-year period. Several Coffeys searching for ancestors, but none from Killybog. Many of the inquiries posted a few years ago still hadn't received responses. Most of them were from people living outside of Ireland. Not very promising. Yet I posted a message.

Searching social media for Coffeys in Ireland would probably be more productive than posting on the forums. Maybe it was time to get back on Facebook. If I was no longer allowing Andy to control my life, a Facebook page would be a step in the right direction. And then I wouldn't feel so lonely. When I was home, my only interaction was with my parents and the mailman, who delivered my daily debt-collection notices.

I had cancelled my page, not merely deactivated it, so I started from scratch, using my first and middle name, Caity Ann, no last name. I entered the required information, then tapped an apprehensive finger against the keyboard.

Even if Andy found my page, it was private, not public. I'd make sure we didn't share the same friends so he couldn't stalk me via them.

I published my page, and panic zipped through me.

After several calming breaths, I gave myself a mental pat on the back. However, my sense of accomplishment was short lived. I needed at least fifty friends so I didn't look totally pathetic.

Ten minutes later, I'd only come up with sixteen potential friends, all of them related, except for Declan. I wasn't sure I wanted to see what was on his page. What if he'd posted the pic of me in the sausage costume, then tagged me after we became friends? My cousin Amber in California was recently married. My cousin Emma worked at an upscale Hawaiian resort. My cousin Lexi was twenty-five and studying for her PhD.

Did I really care to see everyone flaunting their wonderful lives in my face when mine was pretty much shit? I was proud of myself for standing up to Andy by creating a page, but I wasn't exactly proud of my life.

I shut down my computer before I could delete my page.

If Facebook couldn't give the illusion that I led a glamorous, exciting life, what could?

CHAPTER EIGHTEEN

Upon waking up the next morning, my first thought was, *Thank God I'm waking up in my bed and not Declan's.* That I didn't have to do the walk of shame from Declan's room to mine. I'd have regretted it. It wasn't merely about Declan not respecting women by sleeping around, but about *me* not respecting *myself* for sleeping with him. I needed to feel better about myself, not worse. And not having slept with him made me feel a bit better. I'd stood strong despite my physical attraction to him. Although he hadn't kissed me, I assured myself he would have if I'd hung around longer.

I was proud of myself for leaving.

I was also psyched to have learned more about Grandma's family. The thought of touring County Wicklow, my great-grandma's homeland and the filming location for *P.S. I Love You,* caused me to spring out of bed.

I rushed through the shower and ironed my black

cotton pants and my new green sweater. Rachel was allowing us to wear business casual today. I tossed my hair up in a clip and put on makeup, including my Manic Magenta lip gloss, which complemented the sweater nicely.

I headed down to the office, where Declan was gathering up the snacks for the tour. I slipped a bag of Taytos in my purse. We exchanged good mornings. Hopefully, he didn't notice the nervous quiver in my voice. He acted casual, as if nothing had happened in his room last night. It hadn't, yet it kind of had.

Had the near kiss meant nothing to him?

"Here's a copy of the tour itinerary." Rachel gave us each a detailed overview of the day. "The guide will handle everything. You guys are just there in case something happens."

What did she think was going to happen?

"Aren't you going?" I asked.

"No. Gretchen and I are staying here to work on my November meeting. I need to find a hotel today. We'll advance dinner at Powerscourt Estate and meet you guys there."

Not having the constant pressure of proving myself all day would make the tour more enjoyable. Yet I *needed* to prove myself.

"Do you have a copy of the dinner contract and menu?" I asked. "In case you're stuck in traffic or something." I said this with confidence, as if I could manage the dinner should she no-show.

Rachel smiled, looking mildly impressed that I'd requested the contract. She likely assumed I'd filed the hotel BEOs in my binder and never looked at them again. She printed out a copy for me. Would she have higher expectations now that she knew I'd seen the menu and I wasn't going in blind as usual? That was fine. I had all day to memorize the paperwork. I'd be prepared for whatever she could throw at me.

Then my confidence took a swan dive.

Gretchen handled food and beverage. What if Rachel made me tag team with Gretchen tonight?

Declan walked over with the bags of snacks. "I asked the bus driver to spot a half hour early, so I'm going to see if he's here." He looked at Rachel. "Too bad you're not going on the tour, since your great-granny was from Wicklow."

Rachel gave him a questioning look, like how the hell did he know our great-grandma's birthplace when *she* hadn't until I'd e-mailed her late last night.

"I forgot to mention Declan helped me with the research. He's a whiz at it. Researched his grandma's family history." Why did I feel guilty admitting that Declan and I had been alone in his room last night when nothing had happened? One more reason I was glad I'd woken up in my bed and not Declan's. "It only took us, like, a half hour. I e-mailed you as soon as we finished." *Check the time on your e-mail!*

"And I e-mailed my mate Peter in Killybog. He might know some Coffeys in the area."

"Take lots of pictures for me." Was Rachel's disappointed look because she couldn't join us on the tour or that she thought something had happened between Declan and me? "I wonder how Mom's doing, finding out she was named after an aunt she never knew about."

"Yeah, I haven't heard back from her."

"We should get going," Declan said.

We went up to the lobby and exited the hotel's side entrance, greeted by an overcast sky yet a pleasant temperature. The weather report called for a 20 percent chance of precipitation. Same as it had the other days. Being a weatherman in Ireland would be a no-brainer. Every day held a chance for rain.

A large bus sat at the curb. "Ah, grand, it's a thirty-five passenger," Declan said. "It was a sixty-seven seater, but since our numbers lowered, I requested a smaller bus. Better to have more room on the road than on the bus. The Wicklow roads are fiercely narrow."

Great. If Declan lived here and thought the roads were bad, they must be deadly. Luckily, I didn't get bus sick.

A twentysomething, petite blonde walked off the bus. She spotted us, and her blue eyes widened. "Declan?"

"Feck," he muttered.

"I haven't seen you forever. This is utterly mad." She walked over and wrapped him in a big hug, despite the bags in his hands.

Quite mad indeed...

He drew back, looking uncomfortable with her display of affection. "Caity, this is Hannah. We've worked together a few times."

Hannah's hand lingered on Declan's arm, making me question their "working" relationship. Was Hannah possibly one of the *several others* who'd told Rachel stories about Declan sleeping around?

"I'll put these on the bus," she said, taking Declan's bags. "Be right back."

I raised an accusatory brow at Declan. "Another Guinness Girl?"

He shrugged. "Not really."

What was that supposed to mean? That technically they hadn't had sex—they'd just fooled around?

"A *Jameson* Girl." He laughed, but the look in his eyes said *guilty as charged*.

A sense of relief once again washed over me that I hadn't slept with Declan. I'd be going berserk right now. I refused to be another Hannah, and especially not a Gretchen. I refused to be a Guinness Girl. And I needed to be able to stand on my own before I became involved in another relationship. A relationship with a guy I could trust to be faithful, to respect me, and who lived on the same continent as me. My trust would never span an entire ocean. Especially when it came to Declan.

Attendees trickled down and boarded the bus. Kathleen walked up wearing her new brown-and-blue plaid scarf she'd bought on our shopping trip.

"I just love this scarf. Wish we could do some more shopping. Too bad we leave tomorrow."

Tom walked out the door, and my first instinct was to hide. I was no longer supposed to be avoiding VIPs, but avoiding getting fired was a survival tactic. He yawned, and exhaustion weighed heavy on his eyelids, like maybe he'd spent the night on the couch after a heated argument with his drunken wife.

I unzipped my purse. "Excuse me. My phone is vibrating."

I stepped away to answer my fictitious call.

Kathleen boarded the bus, followed by Tom, who smiled faintly, not his usual dynamic self.

It was going to be impossible to avoid them when we were on a bus together all day. Besides, if he wanted to fire me, he'd have done it by now, right?

⚜ ⚜

The tour's first stop was a quaint village where scenes for *Michael Collins* were filmed. Even though I'd never heard of the 1990s movie starring Liam Neeson and Julia Roberts, it was cool to visit my first filming location outside of Universal Studios. Michael Collins, a historical figure in Ireland, had played an integral role in freeing Ireland from British rule and forming an independent republic. I didn't do war or history movies. However, now knowing my Irish connection, I made a mental note to watch it.

The next stop was Glendalough, one of Ireland's most important monastic sites, with many well-preserved structures, including a small church and a round tower jutting up in the middle of a cemetery. Nestled in a wooded valley with two lakes, the area had been a filming location for *Braveheart*. Hard to imagine such a violent movie being filmed in the peaceful and serene setting.

I was traipsing through the cemetery, rounding up attendees, snapping pics of the scenery like a mad woman, when I spotted Tom Reynolds. Besides saying good morning to him and Kathleen, I'd successfully dodged them. I prepared to duck behind a massive tombstone, when he called out my name. I smiled, giving him a wave. My heart racing, I prayed I could answer his question or solve his issue, which hopefully wasn't about me getting drunk with his wife and dissing him.

"I wanted to thank you for taking Kathleen shopping and"—he glanced discreetly over at his wife chatting with another wife—"for taking care of her." I about collapsed with relief that he didn't blame me for his wife's drunken state and that Kathleen apparently hadn't repeated our conversation. "She rarely drinks, but Alyssa going off to school has been tough on her."

"I totally understand. I had fun."

He smiled. "I'll make sure to tell Rachel how much I appreciate you spending time with her."

Could I have that in writing?

I had a feeling he'd be leaving out the part about Kathleen drinking, and I wouldn't be mentioning it either. Rachel had likely kept some dark, blackmail-worthy secrets over the years. A job requirement, no doubt.

I finally succeeded at herding everyone out of the cemetery, only to have two women wander over to a row of souvenir stands. People were in no hurry to board the bus, so I decided to let them browse a few minutes. Rachel's spy approached Declan and me.

"Are we going to be stopping in Blessington?" He directed his question at Declan rather than me.

I knew this one!

"Yes, we are," I blurted out. I recited our detailed itinerary, having already memorized it.

The guy smiled at me. "Great. Thanks."

I glanced over at Declan. "Sorry about cutting in." Especially after I'd gone berserk over him taking charge of the walking tour the other day. "I couldn't believe I actually knew the answer."

Declan shrugged. "You're grand. I didn't have a bloody clue if we were going to Blessington."

I loved a guy who could admit he didn't have all the answers.

"I told you you'd get the hang of the job."

One correct answer didn't really make me competent at my job. Yet I was almost giddy with pride. I was on a roll—answering questions, hunting down a lost cell phone, and averting disaster while escorting the CEO's wife shopping. I'd come a long way since panicking over this guy's question about the boarding pass kiosk at the beginning of the trip.

My phone rang. Mom. I let it go to voicemail. I'd call her back on the bus. Hopefully, she wasn't freaking out over being named after an aunt she'd never heard of. My phone dinged at the arrival of a text from Mom. *Call me immediately!*

I stepped away, speed dialing her. "What's up?"

"I'm in shock."

"Sorry. I thought you'd want to know about being named after Grandma's sister."

"Yeah, that was a surprise, although I think an Ellen might have been mentioned in one of the letters. Several names were, but we didn't know if they were related. But that's not what I'm talking about. Rachel called me."

Silence filled the line.

"What did she say?" I asked.

"She's never called me while traveling for work. And she didn't call because one of you was in the hospital, but just to talk. Supposedly to see how I was doing after your e-mail and to thank me for my mother's photo."

"That's great."

"So what's wrong?" Panic escalated in Mom's voice. "What happened?"

"Nothing."

"I won't tell her you told me. It must be something awful that she felt the need to hear my voice."

"Seriously. Nothing bad has happened. I swear to God."

I didn't blame Mom for being suspicious. I'd have been if I wasn't there to witness Rachel's keen interest in Grandma's ancestry. I hadn't been the best daughter over the past two years, but Rachel had hardly been around since starting at Brecker six years ago.

Declan waved me over—the bus was waiting on me. Hannah stood next to him, laughing at something witty he'd said. I wanted to be the recipient of Declan's humorous story. A tinge of jealousy lurked at the back of my mind, and I shoved it aside.

I marched back toward the bus. "I have to go."

"Oh, and Teri found the letters."

I slowed my pace. "What do they say? Do they confirm Grandma was from Killybog?" I was confident I had found the correct family in the census, but it would be nice to have a document confirming it.

"She's still looking for the naturalization papers, which should have the town my mom was from. The letters don't mention it. She's going to photocopy them next week and stick them in the mail."

The Pony Express could have delivered these letters faster.

"Hopefully, she finds the naturalization papers," I said.

I promised Mom I'd call her later.

Hannah was still giggling. A soft, flirty, somewhat annoying giggle. I joined them by the bus.

"He's so funny." She leaned in, touching Declan's arm. "It's been too long. Ring me sometime. Same mobile number."

I glanced away, unable to watch Hannah blatantly throwing herself at Declan. Did this chick have no shame? No self-respect? Did she not realize she was one of dozens, maybe hundreds? I seriously would not want to be in Hannah's shoes, waiting by a phone that was never going to ring. Unlike Declan, Hannah and Gretchen had obviously expected more than a one-night stand.

Had Declan led them to believe *he'd* wanted more to get them into bed?

Tom Reynolds poked his head out the bus door. "I think that's everyone."

"Yes, it is," Hannah said. As if she had a clue. She hadn't been paying attention to anyone besides Declan.

I peered over at the two women still browsing the souvenirs. "Actually, we're waiting on those ladies."

"Oh, good catch." Tom smiled and ducked back inside the bus.

Hannah shot the ladies an annoyed look, as if it was their fault she'd almost left without them. It sort of was, but it was our responsibility to make sure we didn't leave anyone.

Hannah marched over to the women.

"Have you ever left someone behind?" I asked Declan.

"More than once. And once it was me."

At least I hadn't done that yet.

A few minutes later Hannah returned with the women. She boarded the bus, taking her spot at the front, addressing the group on microphone, while Declan and I sat at the back.

"Is everything all right?" he asked.

What? Am I acting awkward after our near kiss, while you seem unfazed by it?

He gestured to my phone, having been referring to Mom's call. Thank God I hadn't just said that out loud.

"It was my mom. Rachel called her."

His forehead wrinkled in confusion. "Your mom rang to tell you Rachel rang her?"

"She doesn't call much—never when she's traveling for work. When I called to tell her I got into college, which was big news, she was traveling and didn't return my message for a week."

I wanted to ask him when he'd last called his mom if he hadn't been home since Easter. Or was she the reason he hadn't been home? He never mentioned his parents.

He slipped his phone from his pocket as if reading my mind, preparing to call his mom. Instead, he opened his e-mail. "Still nothing from Peter. He's a good mate. He'll get back to me."

Hannah directed our attention to video snippets from *Braveheart* playing on the overhead monitors. "As we drive through Wicklow National Park, you'll recognize scenery from the movie."

Doubtful, since I'd had my eyes closed through three-quarters of the bloody and violent movie so I didn't throw up my Milk Duds. I snapped pictures, more curious about my great-grandma's homeland than the movie.

The bus climbed to a higher elevation, a fairly sharp drop down to the valley. Yet the Wicklow Mountains were more like really tall, rounded hills than steep, treacherous mountains. Although these were my first mountains, so I wasn't exactly an expert. An occasional burst of red, yellow, or orange leaves exploded among the predominantly green ones. Back home the trees had peaked. The land flattened out into a gently rolling landscape of trees, bushes, stone fences, and a few scattered houses. A herd of sheep grazed along a side road. A bright splash of red added color to their cream wool coats.

"What's with the painted sheep?" I snapped a pic.

"It's dye. Designates ownership if they wander off."

"I'd color mine hot pink or purple."

Farther into the park, the bus took a sharp turn and drove up a winding road with an increasing number of houses, as if we were returning to civilization. We rounded a corner, encountering a breathtaking view of a lake below. Hannah held on to a bar, steadying herself.

"So if that was you up there, you'd have fallen down the stairs, huh?"

Declan smiled. "In my defense, I popped right back up and continued my talk, earning a round of applause." He took a faint bow.

I laughed. "I'm sure you did."

Recalling his reference to having almost killed a CEO, I asked him for the story.

"I was working an off-site dinner, and the restaurant was told no pineapple on the menu because the CEO had a fierce allergy. During dinner, he came to me in a panic that his throat was swelling shut, and we rushed him to the hospital. Turned out some rogue bartender was making pineapple cocktails in a blender, which weren't on the menu, and the fruit was airborne. Lesson learned to always check the bars."

"Was the planner upset?"

"She fired me."

"But that wasn't your fault. It wasn't on the menu."

He shrugged. "I took advantage of a few free days in Amsterdam. Had never been to the Van Gogh Museum. You win some, you lose some."

A good attitude to have. After losing my job, I'd stayed in my jammies for two days, watching Animal Planet, my comfort channel, and plowing through two bags of chocolate chips, a container of chocolate frosting, a jar of marshmallow whip, and every other tasty baking ingredient in the house.

I removed that evening's dinner menu from my purse and scanned it. The event cost more than I'd spend on my wedding. If I ever got married. Besides food, there were fees for the venue rental, specialty linens, and floral arrangements. The remarks section noted an attendee with a nut allergy and a pescatarian.

"What's a pescatarian?"

"Doesn't eat meat but eats fish."

"All seafood? There's shrimp and oysters on the menu."

He nodded. "Generally."

I marked the food restrictions with a yellow highlighter. I jotted down notes as Declan walked me through how to "advance" a dinner, checking everything from no spots on the chairs to testing a microphone. Maybe I shouldn't have asked for the contract, and kept Rachel's expectations low.

We turned down a narrow road and drove up a hill along the lake's shoreline. We met a small truck, and the bus slowed down, hugging the shoulder, shrubs and tree branches scratching the side of it. My gaze was glued to the truck's dented hood, mere inches from the bus. After the vehicle safely passed, I let out a relieved sigh, happy I wasn't driving.

Hannah directed our attention to a video clip from *P.S. I Love You*, when Hillary Swank and her friends lost their oars while boating on this lake.

"Great scene," I said. "I'd love to have a pair of purple wellies and row around the lake with my friends. What a cool trip."

Not only did I need money to do that, but also friends. Sadness, and a sense of longing, came over me. I really missed Ashley and our movie marathons. How we could carry on a conversation solely using quotes from our favorite movies and how people would look at us like we were nuts.

The bus driver slammed on the brakes. Declan snapped his arm across my chest, preventing me from head-butting the seat in front of me.

I knew the day had been going too smoothly.

Declan popped up, peering out the front of the bus. His concerned expression relaxed into a smile. "Ah, rush hour in Ireland, folks. Your chance for a few snaps."

A herd of sheep with green splashes across their wool coats was strolling up the middle of the narrow road. The driver pulled into a small gravel parking area for Hugh's Overlook Lounge. Everyone quickly filed off the bus to take advantage of the photo op.

"Please tell me you were kidding the other day about the mad-sheep attack."

Declan smiled. "I was messing with you. But you never know..."

By the time I got off, the group had spooked the sheep, which were trotting away. Declan took several pics of me standing in the road with a dozen sheep butts behind me. We walked over to a grass strip along a stone fence, away from the group. Dozens of sheep dotted the green rolling hills overlooking the lake. A breeze swept my hair across my face and filled my nose with the scent of freshly mowed grass and earth. The many shades of green grass resembled a patchwork quilt Grandma might have sewn.

An overwhelming sense of déjà vu sent a shiver of awareness up my back. I felt like I'd been there before, like I belonged there. It seemed crazy to feel such a deep connection to a place when I hadn't even known my great-grandma's name until yesterday. But maybe her family's sheep had grazed in these fields and she'd swam, or possibly even bathed, in this lake.

Declan took a pic of me with the lake in the background. I clicked Send Photo and typed *P.S. I Love You Lake* in the subject line and *P.P.S. I Miss You.* I paused a moment before typing in Ashley's e-mail addy. I shot it off to her, nervous anticipation zipping through me. What if she didn't respond? Would the knowing or not knowing if she forgave me be more difficult?

"It was so sad she lost the love of her life in the movie," I said.

Declan let out an exaggerated groan. "Just ruined it for me, you did."

"The movie trailer tells that she's a widow. It's not a surprise ending. It's the movie's beginning."

He smiled. "I've seen it. But once was enough."

"Don't like chick flicks?"

"Don't like sad, depressing movies."

"Yeah, it was sad she lost the man she loved, but you know how many people never find a love like that?"

Declan stared out at the lake. "When you lose someone you love, you lose a part of yourself that you never get back." A look of longing filled his blue eyes, and a deep sense of sorrow came over him. I wasn't sure if the wind or sad memories were making his eyes water.

The painful expression on his face caused an aching feeling in my chest. I wanted to reach out and touch Declan's arm, but what if my small act of compassion made him uneasy or caused him to cry? Neither one of us would know how to react.

Or worse yet, what if he pushed me away?

"Like a part of you dies," he muttered, massaging the silver Celtic symbol on his bracelet, still staring at the lake. A car zipped past, spitting up gravel on the side of the road, jarring him from his thoughts. "I really miss my granny."

"There you are." Hannah walked up and placed a hand on Declan's arm, where my hand should have been, like it was the most natural thing to do.

Damnit. Why had I hesitated? I should have reached out to him or provided a few comforting words.

"Everyone is getting back on the bus." Hannah slowly lowered her hand from Declan's arm.

They headed back toward the bus. I trailed behind.

Had Declan really been thinking about his grandma, or a lost love who'd died? Or had the player been played and been dumped by a girl he'd actually cared about, possibly loved? After Rachel's warning about there being *several* women besides Gretchen, and then this Hannah chick, I couldn't imagine playboy Declan ever having been in a committed relationship. Yet, I *could* imagine the considerate and caring Declan I'd come to know having had one.

Did I know a side of Declan that Rachel and others didn't?

CHAPTER NINETEEN

White-gloved waiters in black-tailed tuxes served wine, beer, and fancy hors d'oeuvres on a terrace overlooking the sprawling gardens at Powerscourt Estate. I envisioned the palatial mansion built in the seventeen hundreds having once hosted elaborate balls, with women dressed in long, flowing gowns and men in tuxes, sneaking out to the gardens for a moonlight kiss.

The green Wicklow Mountains provided a panoramic backdrop to the forty-seven-acre gardens with meandering pathways, showcasing colorful flowers and statues. Stairs and terraced lawns led down to a fountain spraying a steady stream of water high into the air. A peaceful and idyllic setting. I was expecting a lady's heel to become wedged in the terrace's stone mosaic design, causing her to break an ankle. Or for someone to lean back on the ornate black iron railing and fall to the gardens below.

I was learning to prepare for the worst.

However, the dark clouds that had earlier threatened rain had given way to a purplish-pink horizon. And the tall propane heaters scattered around the terrace provided a comfortable evening temperature.

The day had gone smoothly. Maybe nothing would go wrong.

"I wonder how much a room here costs," Gretchen said, walking up with Rachel.

"Probably out of Brecker's budget," Rachel said.

I'd read in the paperwork that the estate had closed in the 1970s due to a fire the day before it was scheduled to open to the public. No funds to renovate, it'd become a chain hotel. An upscale one anyway, so it maintained its grandeur.

"Several TV series and movies were filmed here," I said. "Have you ever seen *Ella Enchanted* with Anne Hathaway?"

Rachel shook her head. "I'll have to watch it."

"I'm going to go check on dinner," Gretchen said.

"Actually, I'm going to have Caity do dinner."

"What?" Gretchen and I said simultaneously.

"I'll have you watch over the reception," Rachel told Gretchen.

I'd been upgraded from bathroom attendant thanks to my successful outing with Kathleen and requesting the dinner's paperwork. My heart raced. I was on.

"I'll help you," Rachel said.

My heart raced faster. Rachel and Gretchen had arrived before me. They'd undoubtedly already checked everything, and she was testing me to see if I'd read the details.

"I saw there's a nut allergy," I said. "Should we make sure the chef is aware of it? I didn't see any nuts on the menu, but I know sometimes they can sneak into sauces."

Gretchen looked shocked by my knowledge, and Rachel appeared impressed.

"I double-checked when we got here," Rachel said. "But good call."

Too bad Declan was out front waiting on Flanagan's executives rather than here witnessing his star pupil in action. He'd also put Hannah in a car back to Dublin, or his hotel room, since the tour had officially ended here.

We walked away, and I could feel Gretchen's glare singeing the back of my hair over me invading her food and beverage territory. Maybe her issue with me wasn't about picking up my slack but that she feared I'd be replacing her.

Yeah, right.

"Has Declan heard from his friend about any Coffeys he might know?" Rachel asked.

"No, but Aunt Teri found Grandma's letters." I wasn't sure if Mom had known that when talking to Rachel.

"Yeah, she mentioned that when I called her earlier."

Rachel didn't elaborate on why she'd called Mom or acknowledge how out of character her call had been. Guess she didn't think it was as huge of a deal as Mom and I did.

We climbed up the steps toward the terrace along the back of the mansion, checking the heaters along the way to ensure they were functioning properly. Soft Celtic music and twinkle lights provided ambiance as dusk settled in, and the outdoor lanterns flickered on. Gold-colored overlays covered cream table linens, matching the chair covers. The waitstaff scurried around lighting the candle centerpieces. Green, yellow, and ivory floral arrangements decorated the bar and food buffets.

I smiled at the bartender, a middle-aged guy named Ryan. "Are you serving Brecker Dark and Flanagan's?"

He nodded. "I certainly am, luv. Would you like one?"

I shook my head. "No thanks."

A microphone and compact sound system sat on a round cocktail table tucked behind the bar.

"Should I check the mic volume?"

"I already did. Tom never uses one. It's just a backup. He prefers a more informal talk if we're in a small enough setting."

A chef in a tall white hat stood behind a turkey and beef carving station, and another stood at a sushi station. Silver trays displayed shrimp cocktails in crystal glasses and oyster ceviche in martini glasses. I had no clue what ceviche was or if I liked oysters, but my stomach growled.

"The pescatarian will be happy."

Rachel nodded. "Yes, he will."

Chocolate flowed down a fountain surrounded by accompaniments of marshmallows, strawberries, pound cake, and rice crispy bars.

"Kathleen had macaroons yesterday at lunch. They're her favorite. I saw the restaurant here serves lunch, and there's a food hall. Do you think they might have macaroons?"

Rachel smiled. "Good to know. I'll go check with the banquet captain." She went in search of macaroons.

Ten minutes later, a silver tray with a pastel rainbow of macaroons appeared on the desert table. My first rainbow in Ireland.

Gretchen came up from the reception. "Do you want me to invite people to dinner yet?" she asked Rachel.

"Sure."

Gretchen eyed the macaroons, then me. "Uh, those aren't on the menu." She said this as if she'd caught an error that I hadn't.

"Yeah, Caity mentioned they're Kathleen's favorite, so we added them."

I swore a low growl vibrated at the back of Gretchen's throat as she turned and headed down to the reception.

When dinner was in full swing, Tom Reynolds stood on the top step leading into the mansion. He clinked a knife against his beer glass, requesting everyone's attention. He'd declined a mic, as Rachel had predicted, and his booming voice easily projected across the terrace. He thanked Brecker and Flanagan's employees for their hard work in forging a relationship between the two companies and partnering with Kildare Sausages. He named a few individuals who'd been instrumental to the acquisition's success. Of course, like Rachel, he didn't use the taboo word *acquisition*.

"We couldn't hold these meetings without the help

of our event planner, Rachel Shaw." Everyone clapped, and Rachel gave a little wave. "And her dedicated staff, Gretchen, Declan, and the newest addition to the team, Caity. Nice to have you on board, Caity."

All eyes were on me and my flushing cheeks. Rachel smiled proudly, unlike at Malahide Castle when Tom had discovered we were sisters. Self-confidence welled up inside me, and I stood a little taller, smiling brightly.

Rachel put me in charge of monitoring the seafood display, making sure it was replenished as needed. She informed me that the shrimp was served in individual glasses so people didn't pile it on their plates, causing them to run out. Great idea in theory. However, people were merely taking two and three glasses. Once everyone was seated and eating, I snagged a shrimp cocktail and oyster ceviche and snuck off to our staff table tucked away in a dimly lit corner. I snapped a picture of the six large shrimp hooked on the rim of a crystal stemmed glass containing a pinkish-colored cocktail sauce and lemon wedges on crushed ice.

Halfway through my shrimp cocktail, Rachel received an e-mail. Her eyes widened as she read it. "Shit."

"What is it?" Gretchen asked.

"I gotta go. It's already midafternoon back home. I have to make some calls." Rachel sprang from her chair, glancing over at Declan. "Ask the driver who brought me to pull up out front." She disappeared through the mansion doors, like the clock had struck midnight and her ball had ended.

"Must be bloody awful for her to run off without telling Tom," Declan said.

The expensive shrimp tossed in my stomach.

And there was the storm I'd been anticipating all day.

CHAPTER
TWENTY

The evening was a huge success, except we spent dinner discussing every scenario that might have caused Rachel to flee without a word to Tom. With all of their experience, Gretchen and Declan came up with some pretty horrible possibilities.

I prayed none of them were accurate.

When we arrived back at the hotel, we headed straight to the office to check on Rachel. Things were worse than anticipated. Rachel was pacing, holding a nearly empty wineglass.

I stepped cautiously toward her. "What's wrong?"

"The hotel booked our main competitor in the space next to us for our December meeting. The CEO is Tom's archenemy. No way in hell is he going to hold a meeting in the same hotel as the guy, let alone in the ballroom across the hall."

"Can't they cancel the other group?" Gretchen asked.

"They were contracted first. It seems a contract means nothing though, since ours clearly states no competitors can be booked in the hotel over our dates. And I'm never going to find another hotel in December, with all the holiday parties going on. Tom is going to go ballistic. Fa la la la la." She knocked back the last swallow of wine, and the vein in her forehead looked ready to explode.

"Get your legal department involved," Gretchen said. "It's a breach of contract."

Rachel shook her head in frustration. "I will, but it isn't going to matter unless legal can build a hotel before December. The other group also has a no-competitor clause. I can't believe my sales rep screwed up. She's blaming it on a new computer system and the other group's info not reflecting accurately. A total bullshit excuse."

"It's not your fault anyway," I said.

"Doesn't matter. I'm going to hear about it and be responsible for finding another venue, which will probably be the airport motor lodge at this point!" Rachel flinched, pressing a hand against her right side. She'd had a major kidney infection in college and once mentioned that when she got too stressed out, her right kidney throbbed.

"Are you okay?" I asked.

She gave me an incredulous look, like I'd lost my mind. "Of course I'm not okay."

"No, I mean you're holding your side. Are you physically okay? Is your kidney acting up?"

She snapped her hand away from her side. "I'm fine."

"This isn't worth losing a kidney over," I said. "It's just a job. Don't let it get you so stressed out."

She stopped pacing, and her gaze darted to me. I expected steam to blow out her ears. "*Just* a job? You know how hard I've worked for this position? To manage an entire department? That attitude is precisely why you don't have a job, Caity." Her gaze sharpened. "Probably why you got fired from your last job and I had to give you this one, when I didn't even need more staff."

My body went rigid and heat raced through me. How dare she tell Declan and Gretchen I'd been fired! And that she'd felt obligated to give me this job!

"Well, I don't need your charity or this job. I quit."

"Of course you do. You never stick with anything. You can't even keep a damn car!"

Low blow! I couldn't believe Mom had told her about my car and that Rachel had also thrown that in my face!

Heart racing, I squared my shoulders. "You have no clue why I lost my job. And I can see why you didn't want me coming along on *your* job, because then I'd know what it was really like and how bad your life is when you want everyone to think it's so perfect. Well, it's far from perfect. And seeing how bad it sucks makes me feel better about mine."

Rachel glared at me, hand on her side.

I snapped my mouth shut.

She was obviously lashing out because she was upset and in physical pain. Not that it gave her the right to tell everyone I'd been fired and had my car repoed. But when I should console someone, like with Kathleen and Declan, I had no clue what to say or how to act. And then when I should keep my yap shut, I blurted out all kinds of horrible things. I considered myself a compassionate person, but I lacked the natural ability to comfort people. I didn't react well in emotionally intense situations.

I would make a shitty counselor!

"I'm sorry," I muttered, then turned and marched past Declan and Gretchen, who stared at me in wide-eyed disbelief.

Rachel was right. I didn't have a stellar work history, or a history of sticking with anything, except psycho Andy for two stupid years. I'd hoped to learn a lot from Rachel as far as organizational skills, how to troubleshoot, and to think on my feet. But I hadn't expected to learn what *not* to do.

To not let a job stress you out to the point of kidney failure. No worries there, since I was once again unemployed!

CHAPTER
TWENTY-ONE

Heart racing, I flew into my room, my gaze darting around. I didn't know where to begin. Head into the bathroom and throw up, to rid myself of the icky feeling in my stomach? Start packing? Figure out how to rebook my airline ticket to go home ASAP? Call Mom and get her credit card so I *could* rebook my airline ticket? I didn't even have money to get home!

Even worse, I didn't *want* to go home.

Yet I didn't want to stay here. At least not in this hotel.

I was screwed!

And my debt would only get worse now without a job. I had to get a job! But it for sure wouldn't be in counseling. I dropped down in the desk chair at my computer and reluctantly pulled up the e-mails for Moto Mart and the elf job. It was embarrassing enough that Mom's neighbors knew I'd moved back home and that my car had been repoed, thanks to nosey Margaret. No way was I working at Moto Mart and having every parent in town stop in, bragging about how wonderfully my former high school classmates were doing.

I opened the elf e-mail. The three years I'd worked at the mall, I'd only run into a handful of people I knew. Even if my former high school and college classmates shopped in Milwaukee, most of them didn't have kids and wouldn't stop by Santa's workshop.

I accepted the elf gig.

The sick feeling in my stomach intensified.

I wasn't sure if it was at the thought of wearing that elf costume one more year, or the fact that rather than smelling like peppermint candy canes and sugar cookies, I'd arrive at work reeking of manure, wet dog, and tobacco from driving Uncle Donny's truck. Or even worse, if Andy saw me dressed as an elf, he'd confront me and smugly say, *See, I knew you'd regret leaving me.*

A tear slipped down my cheek, and the warm moisture trailed over my jaw and down my neck.

Why hadn't I listened to Rachel's and Ashley's warnings about him? Ashley hadn't responded to my *P.S. I Love You* e-mail. Granted, I'd just e-mailed her earlier today, but she also hadn't accepted my friend request. I double-checked Facebook to reconfirm she hadn't. I had fourteen friends. My cousin had posted a pic of her and her hubby on their honeymoon in Italy last month, announcing she was pregnant.

Another tear trailed down my cheek.

I deactivated my Facebook page.

Rachel would probably never speak to me again. She hadn't talked to me for days after Izzy had swallowed the Barbie dolls' feet. What about *me* not speaking to *her*? She'd made me look like a complete idiot in front of Declan and Gretchen. She had no right to say those things. I eyed the Coffey coaster on the desk. Even the thought of finding Grandma's rellies didn't excite me. A big reason for researching our ancestry was to reconnect with Rachel, to bring our family closer together. I flung the cardboard coaster, and it sailed across the room like a Frisbee, hitting the wall, dropping to the floor with a dent in its side.

I burst into tears, sobbing uncontrollably, dropping my head down on the desk. My muffled sobs turned into full-blown wailing. I covered my mouth so my neighbors wouldn't call security, afraid I was being murdered. Or maybe I'd be kicked out for causing a disturbance.

I had nowhere to go. I'd have to sit in the Dublin airport for two days, waiting for my flight home. A flight I had to take with Rachel. Hopefully, I could change my seat to the opposite end of the plane. Hopefully, I could avoid her until the flight. Maybe that crappy River Liffey Hotel was within my budget.

Still crying, I hauled Dad's worn, brown leather carry-on bag into the bathroom and swept an arm across the counter, dumping all my toiletries into it. I swung my purple floral suitcase onto the end of the bed and unzipped it. I stuffed my laptop into its bag and tossed it into the suitcase. I scooped up armfuls of clothes from drawers and dropped them in. I yanked shirts and pants off hangers and threw them onto the pile. I snatched my travel journal off the desk and whipped it into the suitcase.

Choking back a sob, I grabbed the bottle of wine off the desk and searched for a clean glass. No clean glass. I uncorked it and drank straight from the bottle. Like a homeless wino on the street. The women at Martha's shelter flashed through my mind. Not because they were winos but because they were without homes, many without loved ones. Some of the women had lived at the shelter for months, still no better off emotionally or financially than the day they'd arrived there.

I suddenly couldn't breathe. Rather than gasping back sobs, I was gasping for air. I slammed the wine bottle down on the desk. I needed air. I grabbed my jacket and luggage, then flew from the room. I rode the elevator down to the lobby and bolted across the marble floor, pulling my large purple suitcase behind me, schlepping Dad's brown leather bag, the worn strap weighing heavy on my shoulder. My jacket hood pulled up over my head so nobody would recognize me, I made a beeline for the front door.

"Caity." Declan's voice carried across the lobby.

Shit. So much for not being recognized.

I sucked in a ragged breath, held it, then slowly released it, trying to calm down as I continued out the front door. A cool wind caught my hood, blowing it from my head. Hair whipping against my face, I peered through a teary-eyed haze, marching blindly down the sidewalk toward The River Liffey Hotel.

Declan called out my name behind me. He finally caught up and grasped hold of my elbow. "Slow down."

I came to an abrupt halt and spun around, freeing my arm from his hand, my brown carry-on sliding down my arm and hitting the sidewalk with a thud.

"Where are you off to?"

"I don't know. Anywhere but here." I didn't want anyone to know where I was staying. I wanted to be alone.

"I'm sure Rachel will give you your job back."

No way was I asking for my job back. Except that would show Rachel that I could stick with something. And I needed money to pay bills this month. More money than the elf job paid!

"She'll cool down and get over it. I've seen her blow up at staff before when she's stressed out. She's gone off on Gretchen. Her golden child."

Too bad I couldn't have seen that.

"You two are sisters. You'll forgive each other."

"I'm not so sure this time." I glanced away, blinking rapidly, my tears evaporating in the brisk wind.

"I'll see if some of my clients need staff for upcoming programs. Might be able to get you some work. Send me your résumé."

"That's really nice, but I don't think I'm cut out for this job. I have no clue what I'm doing, and it's too stressful. I see how it's affecting Rachel."

I was cut out to be an elf.

"That's Rachel's personality. You have the choice to not let the job control you. Besides, as a contractor, when the meeting ends, you walk away, no strings attached. If a client makes me dress up like a feckin' leprechaun, I don't work her meetings again. Have control over your destiny, you do."

Having control over my destiny without others controlling me was enticing. To be able to choose what I did, when I did it, and for whom I did it.

"And you do have a clue what you're doing. Give yourself some credit. Really, what did you do wrong this week? Tripping in front of Tom Reynolds was an accident, and Gretchen gave the wrong room number."

"You knew about that?"

He shrugged, nodding.

Well, he didn't know about the garbage meltdown, or my unprofessional comment to Kathleen at lunch over drinks, or me raiding the gift basket...

"You did a brilliant job tonight at dinner."

I wouldn't say I'd done a *brilliant* job, but maybe I'd done a halfway decent job this week, considering this was my first meeting. Thanks to Declan saving my ass. My shoulders relaxed slightly.

"You did grand taking Kathleen shopping, and with the tour today. You took initiative to learn the hotel BEOs. You had confidence in yourself until Rachel started talking shite in the heat of the moment. Then suddenly you think you're incompetent. Well, you're not. And Rachel never said you were or that you'd done a shite job this week."

Granted, she hadn't come right out and said I'd done a crap job, but she also hadn't shown much faith in my abilities. But Declan was right. I'd had more confidence in myself the past few days than I'd had in a long time. I couldn't allow Rachel to take that away from me.

"If I'd let people make me feel incompetent, I wouldn't be doing this job. You should have seen me on my first meeting. I was bloody clueless. I..." A crooked smile curled the corners of Declan's mouth, and he raked a hand through his hair, gazing down at his shoes. "You probably don't want to hear another one of my stories." He let out a heavy sigh. "At least stay tonight. The room's paid for. Get some sleep, and decide what to do in the morning. I should get to bed. I'm wrecked. I have to be down at four to work departures. And I need your help."

I gave him a look that said, *Yeah, right.*

He reached out and grasped hold of my suitcase handle, his fingers touching mine. A warm feeling washed over me. "I'll have a bellman deliver your bags to your room. Walk it off, and get some fresh air."

I reluctantly released my grip on the suitcase, telling myself I was hesitant to let go because I didn't want to go back inside, not because I wanted to continue touching Declan's hand.

He lifted my leather carry-on bag off the sidewalk. "See ya in the morning." With a hopeful smile, he turned and walked back toward the hotel, pulling my purple floral suitcase behind him.

I wanted to call out to him. To ask to hear the story about his first meeting. I was going to miss Declan's stories. How they made me laugh. Picked me up when I was down. Inspired me. Gave me confidence that I wasn't a complete screwup.

I was going to miss Declan's stories something fierce.

CHAPTER
TWENTY-TWO

After standing outside shivering for several minutes, doing yoga breathing to calm down, I headed back inside the hotel. I walked across the lobby, and someone called out to me from the lounge. Tom Reynolds. Ugh. Just my luck. A group of attendees were sitting in the lounge, boozing it up. These guys really needed to go home and give their livers a rest.

I reluctantly headed over to them.

"We just wanted to thank you for everything you did this week," Tom said. The others chimed in, expressing their gratitude, including Martin Brown, whose cell phone I'd found.

I smiled faintly. "You're welcome."

"Wish I was staying another day," Martin said. "And didn't have to leave at five a.m."

"Your departure's at four a.m.," I said.

His gaze narrowed. "Are you sure?"

I nodded, having reviewed the departure manifest I'd copied from Declan. Martin's name had stood out because of his lost cell phone. I pulled out my phone and opened the updated manifest Declan had e-mailed staff. I showed Martin his departure time.

"The ground company recommends plenty of time because security can be a nightmare, and you clear US Immigrations and Customs here in Dublin."

Martin's eyes widened. "Shit. Glad I ran into you, or I'd have missed my pickup and probably my flight. My wife would have killed me and insisted I'd done it on purpose to miss her family wedding we have to be back for." He slammed his pint. "I better get to bed. Thanks again." He shook my hand, and I smiled, standing a little taller.

I reconfirmed everyone's hotel departure times, advising them to be down fifteen minutes prior and that they were leaving from the main entrance, not the side. Pride welled up inside me.

Declan was right. Maybe I didn't totally suck at my job.

❧ ☙

It was almost midnight when I got back to my room. My bags sat inside my door, thanks to Declan. I poured the wine down the bathroom sink and threw the bottle in the garbage. I took the lavender-scented toiletries off the counter so I didn't forget to bring them home for Martha's shelter. Even if I couldn't be a counselor, maybe one day I could help a woman leave an emotionally abusive relationship. To be at least one woman's Martha.

Right now, I needed to be my *own* Martha.

When Martha wasn't around to give me a pep talk, I allowed people to whittle away at my self-confidence, and lost faith in myself.

If I didn't have faith in myself, no one else ever would.

I was right.

I was strong.

I was worthy.

I would land another job. And then quit the elf job.

I opened my résumé on my laptop. It was pathetic. No way could I send it to Declan. Besides, he'd only requested it to make me feel better. I deleted the babysitting jobs, which I'd only done a handful of times in high school. I kept the elf and gift-wrapping jobs and the executive admin assistant one. Mom guaranteed me my previous employer couldn't disclose I'd been fired. But I'd only worked there ten months. I had no longevity at any job, except the elf one.

I added my current position, or rather, the one I'd just quit. Event planner was a bit of a stretch, but I had no clue what else to call myself. I noted a start date of a month ago and no end date. Still no longevity. I'd heard Rachel talk about her job enough to know some of the lingo and how to word my role and responsibilities.

Assisted VIPs with transportation. And tripped while doing it. *Escorted tours.* Ran by a tour guide. *Executed off-site dinners.* Directing attendees to the bathroom and smoking area. However, I'd gained more experience at tonight's dinner. Hopefully, my skills sounded transferable for jobs other than meeting planning. They demonstrated my ability to take on responsibility and think on my feet.

I noted Brecker as my employer, but actually the company was my client. Declan was self-employed, with likely dozens of clients.

What should I call my company? I could give it any name I wanted and show a start date of when my last job ended, three months ago, instead of a month ago when Rachel had hired me.

How empowering was that?

More empowering than my *Póg Mo Thóin* undies!

I went on Facebook and reactivated my page.

Then I glanced at my suitcase by the door, and my shoulders sank. I was leaving Ireland in two days.

What if I never returned?

A sick feeling tossed my stomach.

What if I never located my Coffey relatives and never made it to Killybog?

Even if I was no longer researching my ancestry partly to reconnect with Rachel, I'd do it for myself and Mom.

I *would* return to Ireland someday. I'd start an Ireland fund, even if it was only twenty bucks a month.

I went on Chicago's and Milwaukee's Craigslist to sell the diamond earrings from Andy. I still had the blue signature Tiffany box they'd come in. They'd retailed at three grand, so I priced them at half that.

My chest tightened at the thought of Andy showing up as the buyer, even though the earrings were basic studs, not a unique design. My breathing quickened. I posted the ad.

No matter what it took, I would make it to Killybog.

CHAPTER
TWENTY-THREE

The following morning, I dragged my butt out of bed at the ungodly hour of five thirty. Even though I'd quit, I'd lain in bed last night, reviewing the busy departure schedule in my head and picturing Declan's hopeful smile that I'd be down. He'd seen off the Browns at 4:00 a.m. I was supposed to be to work at six to assist him. It'd be pretty shitty of me to make him handle departures alone after he'd covered my ass this week, even though he claimed he never got stressed out. It would also be more experience for my résumé. Even more so, I wanted to prove to Rachel, and myself, that I wasn't a quitter. Rachel could send me back to my room if she wanted. I'd hoped to wake up to an e-mail from her, asking me to come to work today. However, I should have sent her an e-mail before bed to make sure she was okay and wasn't in the emergency room with kidney failure.

I washed out my *Póg Mo Thóin* undies in the sink and blow-dried them. I stood in my bra and undies, staring at myself in the mirror, ignoring the dark circles under my eyes.

I was right.

I was strong.

I was worthy.

I was also running late.

I pulled my wrinkled black suit and white shirt from my suitcase and got dressed, no time to iron. I tossed my hair up in a clip, gobbed on mascara, and applied my Manic Magenta lip gloss as I flew out the door, repeating Martha's mantra.

The lobby was dead except for two front desk staff. Declan wasn't there, so I poked my head outside the main entrance. No black sedans in the drive and no Declan. A taxi pulled up, dropping off a guy with luggage. The old Caity would have hopped in and escaped to the airport. But not this Caity.

I also couldn't avoid Rachel.

I headed to our office to look for Declan, my stomach tightening at the thought of seeing my sister. Even if she wasn't speaking to *me*, I had a few things to say to *her*.

I walked in to find her alone at her desk, focused on her laptop. She hadn't taken time to flat-iron her hair, and the natural waves made it look shorter. The bags under her eyes were worse than mine, and her dress more wrinkled than my suit. I'd never seen her with a hair out of place. Had she lost sleep over our argument or the hotel screwing up her contract, rather than kidney issues?

She glanced up from her computer with a faint smile. "Morning."

"Morning." We stared at each other, awkward tension filling the air. "How are you feeling?"

She nodded. "Better."

"I hope it's okay I came down."

"Of course. I was going to call you if you didn't. We need to talk."

"Yeah, we do." And I wanted to get everything off my chest before I lost my nerve. "I'm sorry about what I said. But regardless of what you think, I've been trying really hard this week. Tripping in front of Tom Reynolds was an accident. Granted, I should have told you, but I was embarrassed after you'd warned me not to screw up. And the spa mess-up wasn't my fault." My heart was racing, but I took a calming breath and continued. "I feel like you've been judging me based on my past track record, not on how I've done this week, positive I was going to screw up. That's not fair."

Rather than telling me to take the next flight home, Rachel's forehead wrinkled with apprehension, and she nodded in agreement. "You're right." I about collapsed with relief, and the shaking in my knees subsided. "And I'm sorry about what I said too. That was really bitchy of me. I don't know why you lost your job. But I'll listen if you want to tell me." Concern filled her eyes, and a sympathetic tone softened her voice.

Now wasn't the time or place to discuss Andy, to have a complete breakdown, when Tom Reynolds could walk in at any moment. But I felt when I was ready to open up, Rachel would listen with compassion and at least attempt to understand.

"It's a long story, but I'd like to tell you sometime."

Rachel stood and walked toward me. "I think you

have a lot of potential. You just need to figure out where you belong. Get some solid experience. You did good for this being your first meeting. Sometimes I forget how overwhelming this job can be when you're starting out. Even now, it's not easy. I hope you'll still work my meeting in two weeks."

I wasn't sure if she'd spoken to Mom, who would demand she give me another job, or felt forced to keep me on because Tom Reynolds had publicly welcomed me to the team. However, she must have at least a sliver of confidence in me, or she wouldn't put her reputation on the line. Rachel's reputation was her life. Literally, her kidney.

"Of course I'll do the meeting." I could quit my elf job. I also needed the money and to build up my résumé. More importantly, I wanted to repair the rift between Rachel and me.

"It's at Brecker's headquarters, but you'll be flying solo. I'm going to be swamped planning another meeting, and I'll be out of the office one day doing hotel site inspections."

Rachel had enough confidence in me to put me on a meeting *alone*? Did I have enough confidence to work a meeting alone?

Yes. I did.

"After I got back to my room last night, my side was still throbbing. I thought, this is insane. My job is making me physically ill. I need to take better care of myself. I haven't had a vacation in four years. I'm always traveling for work, so the last thing I want to do is travel for fun. And if I stay at home, I'm constantly thinking about my work piling up. I've lost months of vacation time, which is money down the drain. So I decided I'm taking a vacation. I think Killybog would be nice in the spring. What do you think?"

I wanted to go *now* before Rachel changed her mind!

I smiled. "I'll start saving." *My diamond earrings better sell.*

"Maybe Mom would want to go with us."

Depending on what I discovered about Grandma's past.

Rachel stepped forward and wrapped me in a warm embrace. I hugged her back, unable to recall the last time we'd displayed affection. I fought back the tears welling up in my eyes. I hoped she followed through on the vacation and wasn't merely caught up in the moment, being in Grandma's homeland. Maybe Grandma was the glue needed to put our family back together. I had this strange feeling Killybog held more than the secret behind Grandma's mysterious past.

It held some answers to my future.

CHAPTER TWENTY-FOUR

I went to the lobby, but still no Declan. The gift shop had just opened, so I popped inside for a bag of Taytos. Most attendees were departing early, so there wasn't a group breakfast. I perused the necklaces—a variety of Celtic crosses and symbols, including one matching Declan's leather bracelet and his tattoo. I picked up the necklace box.

"Lovely, isn't it?" the saleslady said.

I nodded. "Very."

"It's the Celtic symbol for everlasting love."

Everlasting love?

"It's formed from two triskeles, which are three-cornered knots. The two triskeles are joined together to form a circle, the everlasting circle of eternity. It represents two people joined in body, mind, and spirit in everlasting love."

Everlasting love?

I could not get past the fact that Declan, who likely had a Guinness Girl in every pub in Ireland, had the symbol for everlasting love tattooed on his arm. And it certainly didn't symbolize his love for his grandma, despite the explanation he'd given for his sudden melancholy mood on the County Wicklow tour.

"Would you like to try it on?"

I shook my head, setting down the necklace. "It doesn't really pertain to me."

"Every symbol has a different meaning." She gestured to the array of necklaces. "There's the trinity knot, the—"

"Looking for one last souvenir?" Declan asked.

I gasped, startled.

He relaxed his forearm on the counter, glancing at the jewelry. I prayed he didn't notice the necklace.

"No, ah, um, I mean, yeah, I'm thinking about a Celtic cross."

"Ah, grand. No hurry. I'll be out front. I have a departure. The car's here. Just waiting on the fella."

"I'll be there in a minute."

He headed toward the door, then turned and smiled. "Glad you came down to help." He walked out.

So was I.

I eyed the everlasting love symbol one last time before snagging a bag of Taytos.

I headed out to the lobby and spotted Declan putting Rachel's spy in a car. The guy was finally leaving, like he'd wanted to do since day one when he'd put me to the test. A test I'd passed in the end.

Declan walked inside, wearing a wide, dimpled smile. "Heard from my mate Peter. He's going to ask around about any Coffeys in the area."

A mix of anticipation and excitement raced through me. "Awesome."

"I can let you know what he finds out when I see you in Paris."

My forehead wrinkled in confusion. "Paris?"

"I contacted my client for a Paris meeting I'm working the end of the month. One of her staff just cancelled due to a family illness, so I recommended you. She wants to know if you're available."

Visions of the Eiffel Tower, couples strolling along the Seine, and Renoir's *Girls at the Piano*—a print that hung on my bedroom wall—flashed through my mind. The thought of croissants and café au lait made my stomach growl. I'd dreamed of visiting Paris since I was ten, when I'd first watched *Charade* and *How to Steal a Million* with Mom, a huge Audrey Hepburn fan.

"It's an incentive trip with tours and dinners. The planner's grand and knows you're new. She just needs a floater. I told her you'd be brilliant."

"I think brilliant is stretching it a bit. A lot."

I couldn't believe Declan had recommended me for a job. I thought he'd merely been trying to make me feel better last night. He didn't want to kiss me, but he wanted to work with me again? Rachel might feel obligated to hire me, but Declan shouldn't. He'd likely never see me again and didn't owe me a thing. He had to believe I was somewhat competent. That was a lot of pressure on me when I didn't know the job. He was putting his reputation on the line by recommending me. Why would he do that? What if I totally screwed up and made him look bad? I needed to gain experience from Rachel before expanding my client base.

"Thanks, but I think I'll pass."

"The pay is great." He gave me an enticing smile.

I desperately needed money. Not only for bills but so I could return to Ireland in the spring.

His smile faded. "I wouldn't have recommended you if I didn't think you could do the job."

I wanted to prove to Mom and Rachel that I could do this job. More importantly, I needed to prove to *myself* that I could do it. That I was capable of landing a job without Mom or Rachel's help, merely Declan's. That I was destined to be more than an elf.

And I wanted to see Declan again.

He made me laugh more than I had in a long time. Made me see the bright side of a bad situation. Had faith in me when I didn't. Even if Declan was a bit of a charmer like Andy, he was unlike him in every other way. He made me feel *good* about myself. He didn't hide his emotions. He could make fun of himself and admit his flaws. Even if Ashley responded to my pic of the *P.S. I Love You* lake, I needed more friends. Declan would make a good friend, just not a good boyfriend. I needed friends more than a boyfriend. I needed to be able to stand on my own before standing beside someone.

My heart raced, a mix of fear and excitement. Were these the same emotions Grandma had experienced traveling from Ireland by herself, no clue what her future held? More than stability and a weekly paycheck, I needed Grandma's courage and adventurous spirit.

"I'll do it," I blurted out.

Declan smiled wide. "Brilliant."

Gretchen was walking through the lobby and

strutted over to us. Her blond hair was styled, her makeup flawless. She'd even taken time to put on a jade-colored eyeshadow that complemented her green eyes. I touched my lips, verifying that I had put on lip gloss.

"I'll see you in two weeks in Santorini," she told Declan, then flashed me a sly, victorious grin. "Can't wait to catch some rays."

Santorini sounded exotic. Like someplace Gretchen would bare her breasts on a topless beach.

"It's going to be a mad week—doubt we'll have much time off," Declan said.

Did he want me to know their trip was for business, not pleasure?

"Well, I'll see you at the end of the month in Paris," I said. "Thanks again for recommending me."

Gretchen's eyes bugged out, unable to believe Declan had recommended me for a job. Even more so, she looked jealous. Did she picture *me* now dressed as a French maid in Paris with Declan? Good. Let her.

"I'll contact the planner, Heather Trotter. She'll want to be booking your air ticket."

Air? My heart raced. I'd never flown by myself. We'd flown nonstop to Dublin, and I'd followed Rachel's lead through the airport, customs, and immigration. What if I couldn't go nonstop from O'Hare and had to connect through Frankfurt, London, or some other insanely huge and busy airport? What if I got lost and missed my flight to Paris? I couldn't be intoxicated while traveling alone. I'd seen the movie *Taken*, set in Paris. I knew all about human trafficking.

Get a grip.

Maybe my car being repoed was a sign that I should be flying to work instead of driving. The flight would only take a matter of hours. It had likely taken Grandma weeks to sail from Ireland to America all alone.

A sense of courage rose inside me. I no longer felt like I was running from Andy or trying to escape my life. Instead, I was attempting to *find* my life.

Hopefully, I didn't become a million-miler before finding my place in the world.

COMING FALL 2016

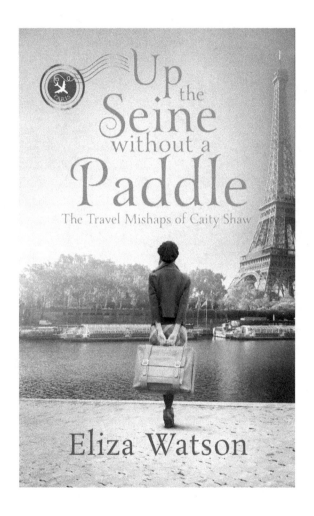

Up the
Seine
without a
Paddle

The Travel Mishaps of Caity Shaw

Eliza Watson

ABOUT ELIZA WATSON

When Eliza isn't traveling for her job as an event planner, or tracing her ancestry roots through Ireland, she is at home in Wisconsin working on her next novel. She enjoys bouncing ideas off her husband, Mark, and her cats Quigley, Frankie, and Sammy.

Connect with Eliza Online

www.elizawatson.com
www.facebook.com/ElizaWatsonAuthor
www.twitter.com/ElizasBooks

9 780989 521970